LOVE BY ACCIDENT

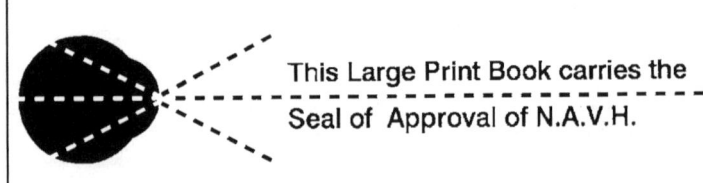

COLORADO CHRISTMAS: BOOK TWO

LOVE BY ACCIDENT

LOVE COMES IN AN UNEXPECTED PACKAGE DURING THE 1880s

ROSEY DOW

THORNDIKE PRESS
A part of Gale, Cengage Learning

Detroit • New York • San Francisco • New Haven, Conn • Waterville, Maine • London

GALE
CENGAGE Learning

© 2007 by Rosey Dow.
All scripture quotations are taken from the King James Version of the Bible.
Thorndike Press, a part of Gale, Cengage Learning.

ALL RIGHTS RESERVED
This book is a work of fiction. Names, characters, places, and incidents are either products of the author's imagination or are used fictitiously. Any similarity to actual people, organizations, and/or events is purely coincidental.
Thorndike Press® Large Print Christian Fiction.
The text of this Large Print edition is unabridged.
Other aspects of the book may vary from the original edition.
Set in 16 pt. Plantin.

LIBRARY OF CONGRESS CATALOGING-IN-PUBLICATION DATA

Dow, Rosey.
    Love by accident : love comes in an unexpected package during the 1880s / by Rosey Dow.
      p. cm. — (Colorado Christmas ; bk. 2) (Thorndike Press large print Christian fiction)
    ISBN-13: 978-1-4104-3097-7
    ISBN-10: 1-4104-3097-9
    1. Colorado—History—1876–1950—Fiction. 2. Christmas stories. 3. Large type books. I. Title.
    PS3554.O89L68 2010
    813'.54—dc22
                                                           2010027663

Published in 2010 by arrangement with Barbour Publishing, Inc.

Printed in Mexico
1 2 3 4 5 6 7 14 13 12 11 10

Dear Reader,

Although I was raised in an Amish/Mennonite family, my parents divorced when I was thirteen. Deeply wounded by an abusive stepfather, I was extremely shy. Through a series of very painful events, I was cut off from my parents for five years. As God healed my wounded heart, my true personality slowly unfolded. Now I love talking to people, making new friends, and sharing my faith.

I had been a writer for years, but had never sold a novel. During this healing time, my books began to be published. My first novel, *Megan's Choice,* was a reader's favorite, and I was a favorite new author with Heartsong Presents. *Fireside Christmas* received four stars from *Romantic Times* and appeared on the CBA best-seller list for three months. Then my historical mystery, *Reaping the Whirlwind,* won the coveted Christy Award in 2001. My last release, *Colorado,* has sold more than 167,000 copies to date. To God be the glory. Great things He hath done.

Because I spent so many years struggling as a beginning writer, I have a heart to help people who have plenty of talent but who need personal guidance to cross the hurdle into publishing. In 2006 I founded

ChristianFictionMentors.com, a twelve-lesson interactive program that guides new writers through their first novel.

My husband, David, and I were missionaries on the tiny island of Grenada, West Indies, from 1987 to 2001 with our seven children. While there, I wrote *Survival Cookbook: For Americans Abroad,* 250 recipes for cooking-challenged Americans who can no longer purchase convenience foods. The cookbook is now in its third printing.

I never dreamed that one day I'd love speaking and even appear on radio and television. God continues to broaden my horizons, and I can't thank Him enough.

Visit www.askroseydow.com to ask me any question you may have regarding the writing life, any future books on my horizon, from-scratch cooking questions, or anything at all. You'll see a date there for my next live interview by teleconference. Or visit my Web site at www.roseydow.com. See you there!

To my son, Jonathan Dow, my in-house idea man.

Chapter 1

Colorado, December 23, 1882

Liza Wainright was covering a large pan of bread dough so it could rise when she heard the first rumble. It sounded like an odd groan, followed by a muffled sound almost like a man's shout. Ten seconds later the floorboards shook beneath her feet.

Her seventeen-year-old brother, Caleb, burst into the cabin, his boyish eyes wild, "Liza, it's the Hogback! Avalanche!"

With a small cry, she dashed onto the front porch of the cabin in time to see the side of Hogback Mountain disintegrate and slide into the valley below. Though almost a mile away, the rumble was deafening, the power horrifying. Ten feet of snow since the first of December, then a warm spell yesterday and today had made conditions ripe for a catastrophe.

Liza stared, unable to move a single muscle. That morning her other two brothers, Bryant and Harvey, had gone to the canyon to check on their cattle wintering there. Every other day the boys had to pull out bales of hay and break the ice on the stream so their longhorns could survive the harsh winter.

So weak she could hardly stand, she whispered, "Did it get into the canyon?"

Caleb's muscular arm circled her shoulder in an awkward hug. His chin touched her right cheekbone though he was only five feet six. "I'll saddle Midnight and ride out there," he said. "If Bryant and Harvey are in trouble, they'll need me." He stepped off the porch and trudged across the ranch yard.

The front doors of the barn and the cabin faced each other, separated by a stretch of earth now covered with eighteen inches of partially frozen snow. As Caleb disappeared into the dim interior across the way, Liza noticed a trickle of black smoke rising from the avalanche area. It grew until it was a wide, dark column.

Heading back inside for her coat, she returned to the porch. She couldn't take her eyes off the sooty plume in the distance. She stood and watched, absently pushing her brown hair behind her left ear where it had sprung loose from her bun.

When Caleb reappeared, he was in the saddle. Liza pointed to the smoke. "Is that a train?"

"Looks like coal smoke," he said. He squinted as though he could peer through a mile of misty morning. "It's got to be a train. I wonder if it got caught in the downfall."

"Check on the boys, then go and see if anyone's hurt," Liza said. "If people are stranded out there, they'll be desperate for help. You'll have to bring them back here." A feeling of deep dread filled her midsection. This was the third bad year for the Running W Ranch, and the larder had barely enough food to last the four surviving Wainrights through the winter. How could they feed a large group of hungry people for even one day?

She hurried inside and took a dozen long steps through the kitchen and dining room, then onto the back porch. In a closet-like room to the left — known to the family as cold storage — a frozen side of beef hung from the rafters. Although useless in summer, this place was mighty handy in winter. Hacking off a ten-pound chunk, she heaved it into the kitchen to chop it up for stew. Despite her five-feet-two stature, she could work alongside women twice her size. She had been hauling and carrying since she could remember.

She partially filled two large pots with water from the pitcher pump by the kitchen counter and dropped the meat inside them. She added more wood to the cook stove to get the oven hot enough for the bread. Narrow and squatty, it was a cast-iron relic her great-grandfather, Matthew Wainright, had hauled into the Colorado foothills more than sixty years before.

Matthew and his partner, Harold Anderson, had framed this cabin with their bare hands and lived in it while they tried to build a herd of longhorns. Even after Matthew married Priscilla Connolly, Harold had stayed on. Later, Harold had also married. He and his bride had lived in a cabin where the bunkhouse stood now.

Coaxing the cranky stove to full heat, Liza wished for the thousandth time that Great-Grandpa Matthew had picked out a nickel-plated Empire stove with a hot-water reservoir instead of this wheezing, gasping iron crate.

Holding her skirts high and to the left, she climbed the loft stairs to search for quilts and woolen blankets. The loft encompassed the entire second story with a small hole cut into the floor for the ladder to come through. It was one large room with a partition at one end for storage.

She found the blankets in an old trunk and threw them down the ladder, carefully climbing down after them.

As soon as the bread was fully risen, she put it in the oven then pulled on boots and her coat. The bunkhouse had been empty for more than a year. She must light the stove and sweep it out in case the worst happened. At least there were eight beds out there that could be used for stranded passengers.

Liza was back in the cabin and eight loaves of bread sat on the table, hot out of the oven, when a rider finally came into the yard. She caught a glimpse of him through the front window over the kitchen counter and hurried out to hear the news.

The rider was nineteen-year-old Harvey, her middle brother who was one year younger than she. He had a smooth, wide face and piercing dark eyes.

A small boy huddled against him in the saddle. All that could be seen of the child was a brown coat and matching hat. He had his face buried in Harvey's chest.

"Train wreck!" Harvey called. "We're having to bring the passengers out on horseback. There's no way to get a buckboard or even a sleigh in there. The trails are too muddy, and the tracks are buckled on the mountainside."

He rode up next to the porch steps. Holding onto the boy by his upper arm, Harvey eased him to the porch floor. "This is Mikey O'Bannon," he said. "His grandmother will be one of the first to come. We promised him that."

"That's my sister," Harvey told the child. "Go into the house, and she'll give you something warm. Your grandma will be coming soon." He straightened and said to Liza, "I'm changing to a fresh horse then I'm off to the neighbors. We've got to have food and blankets for about two dozen passengers. There's no way we can take care of that many ourselves."

Relief flooded Liza. "Good thinking, Harvey," she said. She reached out to the boy. "Hello, Mikey. My name is Elizabeth, but most folks call me Liza. You can, too." She took his hand and led him inside. His freckled face was smudged with tears and grime. She found a clean cloth and wiped his face. He avoided looking directly at her but didn't cry anymore.

Sitting Mikey at the table, she cut him a piece of warm bread and poured milk from a covered pitcher that she brought from cold storage. The child ate like he was starved. The rest of the passengers probably were, too.

"Would you like to take off your coat?" she asked him a few minutes later.

Tucking his chin down, he shook his head. Figuring he was still cold, she didn't press him further.

Liza opened the doors of her meager pantry and took a sack of cornmeal from a shelf. Mush was quick to cook and filling to an empty stomach. The stew would never be ready in time.

The porridge was just thickening when boots thudded on the porch and the door flew open. With a blast of cold air, Caleb came in supporting a small woman who was bent over and trembling. She wore a black bonnet and black cape. Liza rushed to help her into a chair at the dining room table, then found a quilt to wrap around her.

Caleb paused just inside the door, his boyish face looking more man-grown every day. "I'm going to saddle four horses so we can bring back more folks next time. Most of them are still inside the cars, but there's no heat and they're freezing."

"I've got the stove going in the bunkhouse," Liza said. "Harvey went to round up more help."

Nodding, Caleb pulled the door open and disappeared.

Liza turned to the shivering woman and poured her some hot coffee. She told her, "Put your hands around the cup to warm them and breathe in the steam." The woman pulled off her bonnet and laid it on the table nearby. Her white woolly hair was combed back into a tight bun. Coming behind the old lady, Liza hugged her close to lend her own body warmth to the poor trembling creature.

"Thank you, my dear," the woman gasped. "I'm ashamed to be such a baby."

"You're not a baby, Grandma," Mikey said, in clear, round tones. He'd straightened in his seat and was wisely watching his grandmother.

"You're right, Mikey," she said. "I need to stop acting like one, don't I?"

She drew in a full breath of the warm cabin air and lifted the cup with both shaking hands to take a sip. Setting the cup down, she said, "My name is Olivia O'Bannon. Mikey is my son's boy. His mother has been ill, so he came to stay with me for a while. Now we're on our way to take him home for Christmas."

Moving to the chair across the table, Liza introduced herself. "My brothers and I live here alone," she added. "Our parents died of cholera two years ago."

Olivia's seamed brow puckered with concern. "You poor dear. Where were they when it happened? Surely not in this valley. I would have heard of it even as far away as Canton's Corner where I live. I've been there since I married. I plan to die there, too." She took another sip. "Although, today I had my doubts about the dying part. When we heard that mountain shaking loose, I thought it was all over."

Mikey said, "It was all over in a minute, Grandma. Soon as the snow fell down." He raised his pudgy hand and made a diving motion toward the oak tabletop.

Olivia smiled and reached out to squeeze the boy's hand. "How right you are, young man. It was all over in a minute." She looked at Liza, waiting for her answer.

"My parents were on their way to Cheyenne when the cholera took them," she said. "It was an anniversary trip my mother had planned for three years." She bit back the sweeping grief that still choked her whenever she spoke of them.

The concern in Olivia's watery blue eyes held a spark of faith. "God had a reason, Liza," she said. "I know your heart is sore, but God has His own plans about our lives.

Are you a Christian?"

Running her index finger under her lower eyelid, Liza blinked and nodded. "Yes, ma'am. I received Christ when I was about eleven years old. Mama and I joined the Congregational Church in Wiley's Corner. Pa and the boys . . ." She shook her head and didn't finish the sentence.

"We'll pray for them." Olivia finished her coffee and pushed the cup slightly back. Shrugging out of her cape, she said, "Now, tell me what I can do to help you." At Liza's protesting frown, she said, "I'm just fine, my dear. I was cold to the bone, that's all."

"Would you like something to eat first?" Liza asked. "I've made some cornmeal mush. I thought that would be warm and filling."

"That sounds wonderful," Olivia said, smiling at Mikey. "Doesn't it, son?"

His chin touched his chest, then swung high and back down again. "With milk!" he said.

"Of course, with milk," Liza said. She hurried to fill their bowls and joined them in the small meal. Who knew when she'd have time to sit down and eat again.

In a few minutes, Liza stood to fetch a basin and sack of potatoes. "I've got meat stewing. We'll need potatoes peeled. Would you like to do that while you sit here?"

"Of course, child. Anything you need."

Liza found her favorite paring knife and handed it to the older woman. "I need to check the stove in the bunkhouse. I lit a fire out there awhile ago, but it probably needs stoking about now."

Olivia smiled and her face took on a wholesome, sweet glow. "We'll be fine right here, Liza," she said, winking at Mikey, who was leaning onto the table with his knees in the chair, choosing a potato from the sack. Flicking the tip of the knife through a partially sprouted potato eye, Olivia had half the potato peeled before Liza had her coat on.

In the bunkhouse, the fire had almost gone out. Liza lingered a few minutes to blow the coals and coax tiny blue flames from the kindling, then she added larger pieces. Several minutes later, the wood crackled and the first rays of heat came through the sides of the potbelly stove.

Satisfied, Liza bent over to pull the back hem of her flowing skirt between her ankles and up to the front of her waistband. She pinned it there. Buttoning her coat, she headed back to the house. The yard had become a churning mass of mud and slushy snow. It sucked at her shoes and slowed her progress.

She had slogged partway across the yard when Bryant and Caleb rode in, each double-mounted followed by three more horses double-mounted as well. Ten people. Liza hurried as quickly as she could to meet them.

Again, the horses sidled up to the porch. Without stopping for a word with her, the boys headed for the barn to switch out horses. A horse carrying two adults tires after just a mile, and their own mounts had been working in mud since early morning.

Slipping out of her damp, slimy shoes, she left them on the porch. When she reached the inside of the cabin, Olivia was already pouring steaming cups of coffee and shepherding the folks into chairs — eight girls and ladies at the dining room table and two men, a distinguished gentleman with a gray beard and spectacles and a young red-haired drummer, in the sitting room in front of the roaring fireplace.

Mikey had found a box of wooden blocks hidden under the sofa, relics of the Wainrights' childhood. He sat on the braided rug and practiced making towers, clapping when they fell down.

"I'll take care of serving everyone," Olivia

told Liza. "You've done the hard part by cooking all this in the first place. You'll need all your energy getting everyone settled. Who knows how long it will be before we can get folks on their way."

"Does anyone know how many more are coming?" Liza asked.

An older man in a broadcloth suit spoke up. "Ten or twelve men," he said. "Cowpokes mostly."

Liza nodded. They'd have to set up bedrolls in the barn. The tack room had a stove in it. That was the logical place to begin. Of course, some of them would be able to leave before nightfall.

She moved to Olivia, who was ladling mush into bowls. "When Mikey gets tired, you can put him on my bed," Liza murmured to her, nodding to the door off the dining room.

The single bedroom made the remaining open area an L-shape, with the kitchen at the front corner and the dining room table inside the back door. The sitting room was on the front wall, joining the kitchen on the other side. From the kitchen sink or the stove, one could see both ways through the entire cabin, east to west and north to south.

"We're much obliged to you, Liza," Olivia replied. The warmth of her words somehow soothed Liza's sore heart. She suddenly wished that Olivia could stay with her for a while.

When Olivia began serving, a young woman with rouged cheeks and an intricate blond hairstyle threw off her cape and stood to help carry bowls to the table. She had dancehall written all over her, from her kohled eyelids to her dangling earrings. The other woman avoided looking directly at her.

"My name's Charlene," she said, to no one in particular.

"Thank you for the help, my dear," Olivia said with a gentle smile.

Over the next three hours, the remaining passengers arrived to make twenty-three in all. When the first group had finished their coffee and mush, Bryant and Caleb took the doctor and the drummer to the barn to set up sleeping quarters, while Liza led seven women and girls to the bunkhouse.

Heavenly warm air met them when Liza opened the bunkhouse door. She handed a blanket to each of the ladies and let them choose their bunks. "My brother, Harvey, has gone for more supplies," she said. "Is there anyone here who lives close enough to return home?"

Four women raised their hands. Liza nodded. "When the neighbors come, I'll ask about getting you rides out of here." She opened the stove door to shove in another log.

A middle-aged matron stepped forward. She had steel gray hair and wore heavy black boots. "I'll take care of that, missy," she offered. "You've got enough on your hands." She glanced toward her teenage daughter, standing uncertainly among the women. "Sharon will help me."

"So will I," an olive-skinned young woman spoke out. "Don't worry about us, Miss Wainright. You've got enough on your mind."

"Why, thank you," Liza said. "There's a lean-to out the back door. That's where the woodpile is for this building."

She looked around at their weary, anxious faces. "A pitcher pump and some tin mugs are just outside the back door, too. Try to rest. Hopefully this will all be over soon."

A murmur of thank yous swelled toward her.

Embarrassed, she hurried outside. She wasn't used to gratitude and didn't know how to respond to it.

She had just reached the porch steps when a wagon pulled by four straining horses zigged and zagged into the yard. The ruts left behind it bore no trace of wagon tracks.

It was sliding all the way. Who would be so foolhardy as to bring a wagon out in these conditions? Every fifty yards would be a monumental task.

Peering closely at the tall, muscular form holding the reins, she suddenly stiffened. He pulled the wagon close to the steps and took off his hat.

"Good afternoon, Liza," he said. His words sounded relaxed and casual, but his eyes were anxious. "One of Brown's boys came running over to tell us about the accident. Ma thought you could use a few things. With the road so bad, we figured that no one else would be able to get to you with very much."

Liza opened her mouth but no sound came out. The wild driver was young Garrett Anderson, whose ranch bordered theirs. She knew him from school, but the Andersons and the Wainrights hadn't spoken for more than fifty years.

Chapter 2

Liza had never understood why such animosity had existed between the two families for so many years, but her brothers — the oldest one, Bryant, especially — had been in several fistfights on the school playground with Garrett Anderson. They never talked about the bad blood, but everyone for miles around was all too aware of it.

Instinctively, Liza scanned the ranch yard looking for her brothers. What would they do if they came out of the barn and found Garrett here?

While she hesitated, the young man stepped down from the wagon. His black boots sank three inches deep into the mud. He turned toward the buckboard, filled with lumpy objects and covered with a canvas. "I brought some rice, canned goods, flour, and coffee. Blankets, too. Ma sent extra dishes." He looked apologetic. "She asked if you could send those things back when you're through with them."

He glanced toward the house. "Do you want to unload this now?"

Liza finally came out of her shocked trance. "Thank you, Garrett. I'm so glad you came. The boys are setting up sleeping quarters in the barn for the folks who can't leave by nightfall. We have twenty-three people, but some of them will be leaving." She held up her hand, motioning for him to wait as she headed inside the cabin door.

Opening it and leaning in so her head cleared the threshold, she said, "Has anyone here finished eating? We could use some help unloading a wagon."

Four cowboys stood up. One was tall and lean, the other three were shorter and of stocky build. They all wore the stoic expressions of Western outdoorsmen. Without a word, they marched outside and within seconds had formed a lineup to get the goods onto the porch.

Soon, two more men came out to help. Liza marshaled them to carrying boxes and crates to the kitchen, where Olivia and Charlene began unpacking them. The blankets, they piled onto the sofa.

Joining the women in the kitchen, Liza fought back a growing lump in her throat. Here was abundantly more than she could have ever asked or imagined.

She was setting canned peaches on the pantry shelf when she heard loud voices outside and rushed out to see what was happening.

Garrett had backed the wagon to the edge of the grass and unhitched his two horses. He was standing between them, holding their bridles. Bryant stood in mud ankle deep not far from the barn door with his shoulders back, chest out, and his face like stone. "I thought you knew better than to come on my land," he ground out.

Liza flew to the porch steps. "Bryant, he came here to help us," she called. "He brought a wagonload of food and blankets. He could have stayed home, Bryant, but he didn't! He fought that wagon through the mud all the way here. How can you be so unreasonable as to send him away? The least we can do is let his horses rest and give him a cup of coffee." She got into a stare-down with her brother and didn't flinch.

The horses sensed the tension and bobbed their heads. Garrett had a job of holding them down.

Finally, Bryant turned and headed back into the barn. Caleb appeared at the barn door for just an instant, then disappeared again.

Liza turned to the group of cowhands hovering on the side of the porch. "Would one of you mind taking his horses to the barn?" she asked. "We should have some neighbors coming in sometime later this afternoon. They may be able to give some of you rides out, if you want. Meanwhile, the men are setting up a bunk room in the barn if you'd like to lend a hand."

To Garrett she said, "You can leave your boots here and come inside."

Despite what she said to Bryant, she had never cared for Garrett Anderson herself. He had teased her unmercifully from the time she was six years old and he was seven in Wiley's Crossing Grammar School. Dipping her pigtails in the inkwell was the least of her problems when it came to Garrett Anderson. But right was right, and the man had done them a great service.

When they stepped inside the cabin, Garrett was the only man present. Liza introduced Olivia and her grandson, but before she could address the young woman, Charlene stepped forward with a wide smile.

"I'm Charlene," she said, offering him her hand. *"Enchanté."*

He awkwardly shook her hand and immediately dropped it. "Ma'am," he said, removing his Stetson.

The resemblance between Bryant and Garrett was immediately obvious. Both men stood just over six feet tall with a full head of hair that was curly and dark; although Bryant's hair was dark brown while Garrett's was a glossy black.

Taking his coat, Liza said, "We just finished feeding everyone cornmeal mush and coffee. I've got a few slices of fresh-made bread, also. Would you like some?" She hung his coat on a peg and took off her own to hang next to it.

"Coffee and bread sound great to me," he said, scraping back a chair at the table. Watching her pour the black brew, he added, "I came to help, Liza. I can chop wood for you or peel potatoes. It doesn't matter much to me."

As Liza set the cup before him, Olivia brought the plate of bread and put it on the table. "You'd be smart to take him up on that," the older woman said. "Even if it's just to help carry things for the kitchen. Those cowpokes are willing enough, but they're pretty nigh useless when it comes to kitchen work." She eyed Garrett. "Of course, you may not be much better."

He grinned at her. "You may be surprised, Miss Olivia."

Mikey ran up to the table with three

blocks balanced between his hands against his chubby chest. He set them down and ran back to the living room for more. While Garrett drank coffee and munched down three slices of bread, the little boy stacked blocks.

"Do you know how to make a wall?" Garrett asked.

Mikey shook his head.

"Let me show you." Garrett placed five blocks in a row with wide spaces between them. Mikey watched intently. Garrett made a second row of four blocks by stacking them over the gaps, then a row of three, two, and one.

Mikey clapped his hands. "Look, Grandma! A wall!"

Garrett laughed. "Now you make one."

Immediately, Mikey's hand shot out and knocked it all down. With intense concentration he rebuilt it.

"That's great, Mikey. Maybe one day you'll be a carpenter." Garrett picked up his plate and cup and carried them to the dishpan where Charlene was washing bowls.

She gave him a sidewise look. "Thank you kindly," she said.

Garrett did not return her smile. "You're welcome, ma'am," he said. He turned to Liza. "Where would you like me to start?"

he asked.

"We need firewood split," Liza replied, a bit shy at giving him chores. "I've been emptying the kitchen wood box with all this cooking." She pointed toward the back door, just three feet from his chair. "The wood pile is out there."

He stood. "I'll fetch my boots and carry them out back to put them on," he said. Pulling on his coat, he opened the door to lean out and snag his boots. Liza held her breath, watching those muddy soles hovering over her floor. So far, the mud had been kept at bay with everyone removing footwear at the door.

When he closed the back door after himself, one of the matronly ladies asked Liza, "How can we help you?"

"We're chopping vegetables to put into the stew for supper," she said. "But the bread is all gone. We'll have to make some more."

"And biscuits," Olivia added. "Biscuits for supper and bread for breakfast. How's that sound?"

"Biscuits would be better for tonight," Liza agreed.

Charlene spoke out. "I make some mean biscuits," she said. "If someone will carry that burlap sack of flour to the table and find me some lard, I'll take care of that deal."

Olivia said, "You know, there will be people trailing in and out of here all day long with folks coming in to help. It wouldn't hurt to go ahead and make a pan or two of biscuits now to feed those hungry souls who ride in." She glanced at Liza. "Don't you think so?"

Liza nodded. "Olivia, God put you on that train to help me get through this. I'm so befuddled at the moment that I can't put two thoughts together in a straight line."

The older woman smiled. "You're doing fine, my dear. Just fine."

At that moment, a man's voice hurrahed the house. Liza grabbed her coat and hurried outside.

It was Miles Henshaw, one of their closer neighbors who lived only two miles away. He had two packhorses with him.

"We heard you have some trouble here," he said, staying in the saddle. "The missus sent some things to help out."

Liza said, "We've got twenty-three people here. Thank you so much for coming. If you can bring your pack horses close to the porch, we'll unload them."

Garrett stepped forward. "Howdy, Henshaw," he said.

The rancher looked at him in surprise. "Garrett. Good to see you."

Reaching for the first box, Garrett said, "I just got here with a wagonload of goods. I wish I could carry some of these folks out of here, but the road is too muddy. I slid most of the way here. If it hadn't been that I hitched my two strongest plow horses to the buckboard, I never would have made it."

Henshaw dismounted and untied the parcels. "There was another avalanche northeast of here, so this section of the tracks is cut off. No trains running for weeks, maybe months. Anyone leaving the area will have to go by horseback. With the snow melting so fast, we're looking at flood conditions in the next day or so."

Liza lifted a canvas sack of coffee. "If you can take a few out on these pack horses, that would be wonderful," she said. "Several people here are from Wiley's Corner or they have family nearby where they could stay." She lifted a tin. "It's a shame this had to happen so close to Christmas."

"Of course," Henshaw said. "I'll be able to mount two of them. If you don't mind, I'll take back a couple of those blankets to pad the horses' backs. I wish I had thought to bring a couple of saddles."

Before they had finished unloading Henshaw's goods, two more ranchers arrived and Harvey with them. Several cowhands trudged from the barn to help with the unloading. The passengers were sorted and labeled according to who could leave and who had no place to go. More coffee was served. Dozens of biscuits were devoured and dishes washed.

When suppertime came, they were left with fifteen passengers at the ranch, including seven cowhands, Dr. Samuel Grotz, and young Joshua Minnick, who sold brushes along the railroad towns. Among the women left were the matronly woman and her daughter, the olive-skinned young woman, Olivia, and Charlene. Mikey, of course, remained with his grandmother.

Garrett stayed busy. He chopped wood for the kitchen stove and carried hot water to the bunkhouse so the ladies could wash up. He found some straw to put on the porch to keep some of the mud out of the house and kept all the fires alive — even at forty degrees outside, the cabin stayed cold. It seemed like Garrett Anderson was everywhere Liza looked.

The group gathered in the cabin for the evening meal, nineteen people to eat with only thirteen seats in the entire house.

Bryant and Harvey found some boards in the barn and nailed together two rough benches to put along the walls of their sitting room. Everyone was elbow-to-elbow and knee-to-knee, but no one seemed to mind.

No one, that is, except Bryant. He was fine with the railroad refugees, but he avoided Garrett with obvious disdain. Liza ignored her oldest brother. As long as there weren't any words, she would wait out Bryant's bad mood until Garrett went home and things got back to normal.

Seated at the dining room table, Joshua Minnick said, "This is great stew, Liza. You're a good cook."

Liza shook her head. "Not me. That's what is known as gang stew. A whole gang of people helped to make it." She held up a large cloth-lined basket piled with golden biscuits. "Anyone want more biscuits? These are gonna get cold and stale before morning."

A grizzled-faced cowboy named Cody drawled, "I'll take that basket, Miss Liza, and thanks to you."

She passed the basket to Garrett next to her at the table and it made a trip around the entire room. When it returned, two lonely biscuits lay on the bottom. Garrett palmed them. He smiled at Charlene. "Looks like you've got yourself the job for the duration," he said, biting into one of them.

She beamed at him. It was the first natural look she'd shown since she arrived.

Liza said, "Where are you from, Charlene? I mean originally." The girl couldn't be much more than Liza's age.

"My folks have a ranch near Austin, Texas," she said. Looking uncomfortable, she lifted her fork to her mouth.

"I went to Austin once to a big horse auction," Garrett said. "My dad took a string down there to sell. He wanted some fresh stud stock, so he traveled all the way to Texas looking for new blood. That's when he got the contract with the army." His voice trailed off as though he was unsure whether he should give out personal information in hostile territory.

Charlene brightened. "You raise horses?"

Garrett nodded. "Morgans."

"We raised a few ourselves," Charlene said. "But the ranch was mostly beef cattle. My daddy said it doesn't hurt to diversify in case the market drops."

One of the cowboys spoke up. "He was right about that. Last summer the bottom dropped out of the beef market, and we've all been hurting ever since." Several men nodded.

Bryant spoke for the first time. "This is the third year we've had rotten luck."

Joshua said, "You aren't the only one. My business has dropped because the cattle business is bad. Who wants to buy brushes when they need food?"

The conversation continued along those lines for several minutes. Finally, Cody mentioned a game of checkers.

Caleb said, "There's a board and some checkers in the tack room. Harvey and I made them when we were kids." He rose from his seat on a bench and set his plate and cup on the table. "I'm sure I can find them without any problem."

With that, most of the men, including Bryant, headed toward the barn. The ladies stayed to wash up and then drifted out, also. Olivia lingered in the kitchen to fill a pot with beans for soaking overnight.

When Charlene said good night, Olivia hugged the girl. "Thank you for your help today, dearie," she said.

Charlene received the hug but acted self-conscious afterwards. Wrapping her cape about her, she carefully lifted her silk skirts before she even opened the door. How she could reach the bunkhouse without ruining that dress was anyone's guess.

The doctor excused himself and headed for the barn, but Harvey lingered. He sat at the end of the table for a few minutes without saying anything.

When Garrett returned to his seat there, Harvey said, "There's a place for you in the loft, if you want it, Garrett. You can't go home with your wagon this late. It's full dark out there."

Something around Garrett's eyes tightened. "Thank you, Harvey. I'm obliged." His words were softly spoken, but somehow they had a hardness to them.

Without another word, Harvey headed for the loft stairs and climbed out of their sight.

Olivia and Mikey were in Liza's room settling in for the night. Liza now occupied her parents' room with their oversized iron bedstead. There was plenty of space on the massive feather tick for two small women and the boy.

"Would you like some more coffee?" she asked Garrett.

With a slight shake of his head, he said, "No, thanks." He rubbed his lower lip with his little finger. "Would you mind sitting here with me for just a few minutes?" he asked. "There's something I need to say."

Fighting back a rising tide of suspicion,

Liza found a chair some distance away and sat down.

Garrett hesitated, then said, "My mother sent me over today. Since Pa had that heart attack last year, she's been wanting to speak to you, but she hasn't known how."

"To me?"

He nodded but didn't meet her eyes. "She feels bad about the . . . discord . . . between our families. She says that nobody knows why the feud ever started, so we should settle our differences and make peace."

Liza said, "I'm not sure if that's possible. You saw how Bryant feels about . . . anyone from your family. I don't know what it would take to overcome that."

"Ma says that Christians shouldn't have such bad feelings between them." He looked at her for the first time. "Your brothers aren't believers, Liza. I know you can't answer for them, but what about you? Can you forgive us? Can you let us forgive you?"

Chapter 3

Liza had always considered Garrett Anderson a boor of the first level. Now that she'd actually talked to him, she wasn't so sure.

They did belong to the same little church. She saw Garrett Anderson every week unless sickness or rough weather kept one of them away. He was the guy who set up the benches, passed out the hymn books, and stood up to take the offering — a fixture that everyone took for granted, at least Liza did.

"God commands us to forgive, Garrett," she said, swallowing and pulling at her skirt seam beneath the table. "I know it's my Christian duty." She finally found the courage to look at him.

"But?" he probed, watching her closely. His brown eyes were deep enough to drown in.

She didn't want to say it, but she had to. "You made my life pure misery when we were in school, teasing me all the time. I used to dread going because of you. I have a hard time forgetting that."

His expression grew pained. "I was too high spirited in those days. I should have had more sense." He leaned closer. "Can you please forgive me?"

He waited for her answer, a softly pleading look in his eyes.

Something inside her melted. She cleared her throat. "I do . . . forgive you. It was wrong of me to hold a grudge."

"Friends?" he asked, smiling kindly.

She nodded and smiled back, willing but still troubled. "I wish I could speak for the boys," she said. "I agree with your mother that there's been too much bad blood between the Wainrights and the Andersons. I wish we could call a truce and forget the whole thing . . . whatever it was."

He grinned at her. "At least we've made a start," he said.

The next morning Garrett came down from the loft within five minutes after Liza reached the kitchen. His curly hair was a mop on top of his head and made him look fifteen years old.

"Would you like me to fetch you some wood?" he asked her. "I can take care of building the fire, too, if you'd like."

"Thank you, Garrett," she said. She pulled on her coat to go outside to cold storage. When the last of their helpful neighbors had left yesterday, the back-porch pantry was crowded, the kitchen shelves overflowing. She had to leave one burlap sack of flour and another of cornmeal propped in one corner of the kitchen for lack of any other place to put them.

Shivering, she brought back a long slab of bacon and set about slicing it. Olivia appeared soon afterwards, every hair in place though it was only four thirty a.m. Next to her, Liza felt scruffy, but she had too much to do to spend more than five minutes dressing. There would be fifteen hungry people at her door before much longer.

"I'll take care of the coffee," Olivia said, reaching for a large cooking pot. The family coffeepot was far too small for this size crowd.

"I wonder if Charlene will come to make some more biscuits," Liza said. "The Craddocks sent a big basketful of eggs. We can have those this morning."

"I'll take care of the beans," Olivia asked. "They can simmer all day. We'll make lots of cornbread, and that'll make a good supper tonight. Cheap and filling is our motto around here."

Liza chuckled and gave the older woman a hug. "What would I have done without you?" she asked.

Olivia cleared her throat. "One of the other women would have stepped up," she replied, smiling. "You would have been fine."

When Garrett had the cook stove roaring, he moved into the living room to add logs to the fireplace.

Liza was frying bacon when she first heard Bryant's voice, loud and strident, coming from the bottom of the loft steps. "I'm not sure what you're up to, Anderson," he ground out. "But I want you off my place by nightfall, you understand?"

"If that's what you want, Wainright," Garrett replied, tightly.

Liza marched to the living room to see Garrett squatting in front of the fireplace with Bryant standing over him. "Bryant!" she said. "How ungrateful can you be? Garrett brought us a wagonload of food and supplies through an awful muddy mess. He could have stayed at home instead, you know. And he's been working without a break ever since he got here." Her lips formed a determined line as she bore in on her older brother. "How dare you speak to him that way!"

"Liza, I'm still the man of the house, and don't you forget it!" He grabbed his sheepskin coat from its peg and slammed out of the house.

Immediately, a shrill cry came from the bedroom.

"I can't believe him," Liza fumed. "He woke up Mikey."

Olivia hurried into the bedroom to soothe the frightened little boy.

"I apologize for him, Garrett," Liza said, her face flaming.

"It's not your fault," he said, dusting his hands off and standing. "I'm afraid I'm as much to blame as Bryant is. I did my share of picking fights when we were in school."

A boyish voice came from the top of the loft ladder. "I'll say you did," Caleb said, climbing down into view. "I remember that, even if I was only seven years old back then."

He stepped off the ladder and gave his sister a hard look. He jerked his head toward Garrett. "Liza, you'd best be careful how you talk to him. Bryant's already sore." He reached for his coat. "I'm going to help with the chores." He yanked the door open and strode out.

Liza stepped over to close the door properly, then let out a discouraged sigh. Suddenly, the smell of burning bacon made her fly back to the stove.

The door opened again, and Charlene stepped in. Her face was free of all traces of powder or rouge. She wore a denim dress and carried a pair of black shoes in her hand. "Good morning, all," she said, a shy cheerfulness in her voice. "I wore my boots over and carried my shoes. It's still a pond of mud outside."

"Maybe it'll freeze over," Garrett said wryly. "Then we can skate to the barn and back instead of swim."

She gave him a wide-eyed smile. "And that would be better?" she demanded, a lilt in her voice. She sat in a wooden chair to slip her stockinged feet into her shoes. "I came to see if you needed help," she told Liza.

"I was hoping you would," Liza said. "Would you mind making more biscuits? They were a big favorite last night."

"My specialty," she said, standing. "If you'll move that sack of flour to the table, Garrett, I'll get started."

Olivia came out of the bedroom. "He went back to sleep," she said. "Poor thing, he's really exhausted. Too much excitement by far."

"I'm sorry, Olivia," Liza said. "Bryant

didn't think about a child sleeping in the house."

"It's not your fault, honey. No harm done," Olivia said, lifting the lid on the pot of coffee. "Does anyone want an early cup of coffee? It's ready."

A chorus of *me*'s rose up. She chuckled. "That's what I figured." She found four cups, and they sipped while they worked.

"Today's Christmas Eve," Olivia said as they dished up eggs and set platters on the table.

Liza let out a gasp. "Christmas is tomorrow! I forgot all about it! Do you think some people may have to stay over that long?"

"If the weather stays like this, Mikey and I will," Olivia said. "I haven't ridden a horse for thirty years. I don't think I can start now."

Charlene spoke up. "I was going to spend the holiday with a girlfriend in 'Frisco. There's no point in going out there now. Traveling by stage to the next train station, I'd get there after everything was over. My next gig doesn't start until next week."

At the word "gig" everyone in the room focused on Charlene.

Noticing the attention, she said, half apologetic, "I'm a dancer," then blushed at her admission.

Liza set the bacon on the table and said, "The boys and I hardly do anything for Christmas. No tree or presents, usually. But we ought to do something special for those who have to stay over. It's awful being stranded when you could have been with your family for Christmas."

Olivia said, "We have plenty of food and plenty of hands to cook it. Why don't we make a big Christmas dinner?"

Liza warmed to the idea. "The Henshaws brought a couple of wild turkeys. We could thaw those out."

Garrett added, "I love cornbread dressing. Does anyone know how to make that?"

Olivia gave an unladylike grunt. "Since I was ten years old," she told him. She turned to Liza. "After breakfast we'll look over the pantry and plan a menu. How about that?"

Liza smiled. "I was dreading another dreary Christmas. Now I can't wait. It's going to be fun."

By six o'clock the entire group had gathered in the cabin for breakfast. When they had all been served, Bryant stood. "We're going to make two runs into Wiley's Corner today," he said. "We can saddle as many as five horses at a time. Those who have no place to go besides a hotel room are welcome to stay. We have plenty of food and the quarters aren't too uncomfortable, are they?"

"They're warm and dry," Joshua Minnick said. "What more could we ask?"

Words of approval came from every side of the room.

"How many can leave today?" Bryant asked.

Ten hands went up.

"We'll set out after breakfast. You'll have to decide among yourselves who will be in the first group." He sat down and picked up his coffee cup.

A buzz rose among the passengers.

"You can go ahead," the olive-skinned lady told the matron and her daughter. "The only place I have to go is back to the boardinghouse. It won't matter if I get there in the morning or evening. You have a family to think of."

Dr. Grotz said, "I don't mean to put myself forward, but I've got patients to attend to. I was only going to a day-long conference, and I should have been back last night."

"You're going, Doc," Bryant said. "No question about that."

Finally, they divided themselves into two groups. The first group — two women and their daughters, plus the doctor — left the cabin to get their things together. The remaining ladies — the olive-skinned beauty, whose name was Rosita, plus a red-haired woman named Ginger and her teenage daughter Betsy — stayed in the cabin to help clear away the remains of breakfast.

Before the first plate was washed, Mikey came stumbling from the bedroom. His straw-colored hair stood up on one side.

Olivia hurried to pick him up. "Well, you finally decided it was tomorrow, did you?" She hugged him, and he rested his face against her shoulder, surveying the world from his privileged perch.

Charlene scraped and stacked plates at the table. Speaking to no one in particular, she said, "We should have a Christmas Eve party tonight. Play some games, have some fun. Don't you think?"

Rosita said, "That sounds like a good idea. Of course, I'll be gone by then, but for those who must stay."

Liza finished pouring bacon grease from the cast iron skillet into a tin can on the back of the stove. She looked up and said, "That sounds nice. I'll ask Bryant if we can use the barn, though I don't see why not." She scanned the faces of the women, looking for volunteers. "We ought to set up an entertainment committee to think of activities and organize everything."

Charlene said, "I'll do that." She looked at young Betsy. "Would you like to help?"

Before her daughter could reply, Ginger shook her head in a commanding gesture.

Charlene flushed but didn't give any other sign that she'd noticed. She turned to Rosita. "Would you help me before you leave this afternoon?"

"Of course." Rosita turned her back on Ginger and scrubbed the plate in her hands with a vengeance.

As soon as the dishes were dried and put away, Charlene and Rosita moved into the living room to discuss the party while Ginger and Betsy worked over a large basin filled with bread dough. Mikey had his blocks out on the rug, but he soon tired of them and began distributing them to every adult in the room calling out, "Special delivery," for each one.

"They're leaving," Rosita called out, bending to peer out the window.

Everyone headed to the porch to say good-bye. With Bryant in the lead and Caleb bringing up the rear, they rode toward the road in a single file. The horses' hooves disappeared into the mud, then reappeared with a squishy sucking sound. The doctor tipped his hat as he passed the porch.

"Thank you, Miss Liza," he said. "You've been wonderfully kind to all of us."

"My pleasure," she said, smiling and waving.

When they disappeared around the bend, the others went back inside, and Garrett came to stand next to Liza on the porch. "Do you want me to go home?" he asked. "If you do, I'll ride one of my horses bareback and lead the other. I can fetch the buckboard later."

"Do I *want* you to go?" She had to strain her head back to look him full in the face when he stood this close. "I can't say that I do, Garrett. Honestly, I don't know what I would have done without you yesterday or today. My brothers are never so quick on the draw when it comes to helping in the house. I'll need a man's strong back to help now and then as long as these people are here."

She sent an anxious glance toward the barn. "I don't want you to go . . . but . . ."

"But your brothers," he finished. "If I told you that they don't bother me, what then?"

"Won't your mother miss you?" she asked. "It's Christmas."

"She sent me over here. She gave me orders to stay as long as I'm needed." He looked serious. "That's why I'm asking you."

"Do you want to stay?" she asked.

"If you want me to, then I want to." He chuckled. "Your turn. Try to break the stalemate, will you?"

A smile forced itself out, and she gave up. "Could you at least stay for the Christmas Eve party tonight?" she asked. "After all this work, you deserve to be in on the fun."

He grinned and his face lit up. "I was hoping you'd see it that way," he said.

She turned to go into the house, and he fell in step with her. "Liza . . ."

She paused beside the door and looked up, waiting for him to go on.

"You know why I used to tease you so much in school?"

He had her full attention as she waited for the answer.

"You're the prettiest girl in these parts, and I wanted you to notice me."

Chapter 4

Garrett's lips pursed out in a rueful grimace. "I guess I got what I wanted, but not exactly as I'd planned."

Liza's cheeks were on fire. Moving away from the door, she walked to the side of the porch that faced away from the yard. If anyone saw her blush, she'd be mortified.

"Did I upset you?" he asked anxiously, coming behind her.

She shook her head. "Surprised, not upset," she said. She drew in a long breath and swallowed. Finally, she turned to him. "Thank you, Garrett. That's the nicest thing anyone has ever said to me."

His brown eyes held a soft light. "I meant it."

Suddenly, Liza forgot she was tired. Suddenly, her feet felt light, and her heart hummed a tune.

Harvey appeared in the barn doorway, and Liza said, "We'd best go inside."

The cabin was bustling with bread-makers, bean-stirrers, and party-planners. Liza set out the turkeys to thaw and discussed lunch options with Olivia. Garrett split wood out back and kept the fires burning. Liza didn't talk to him again for several hours, but she was constantly aware of his presence as he moved from the fireplace to the cook stove, supplying the fires' insatiable appetites with fuel. His warm looks told Liza that he was aware of her, too.

How could this be happening? She'd always dreamed of catching a young man's eye, but Garrett Anderson's? That she'd *never* dreamed of.

Despite Bryant's disapproving presence, they managed to accidentally sit together at lunch, and they lingered over their coffee cups when everyone else was through.

The second group to leave would be Rosita and four of the cowhands, Bryant and Harvey acting as escorts and bringing the Running W horses back.

"I'm sorry to leave you all with the dishes," Rosita said, swinging her long wool cape around her shoulders.

"You go ahead, dearie," Olivia told her, propping the stirring spoon on a plate beside the stove. "Once those men are ready to leave, they won't want to wait. You'd best put your things together in a hurry." She came over to hug the young woman. "God bless you, my dear."

"Thank you," she said. Turning to Liza, she added, "I almost hate to miss the party." She included Charlene, at the dishpan, in her smile.

Charlene gave her a sudsy wave.

Liza stood to see Rosita to the door. "I hope you reach your family soon," she said, glancing into the yard. "Be careful out there. It's looking wetter and more dangerous all the time." She watched Rosita gingerly step into the muddy swill, then closed the door against the breeze. It must be more than forty degrees out there. Maybe the sun and the constant wind would dry out the yard a little.

When she returned to her seat next to Garrett at the table, she said, "I feel like a slacker, sitting here and watching all of you so busy."

"You deserve a rest," Ginger said. "Betsy and I are going to the bunkhouse for an hour or two when we finish here. We'll have some time to rest then."

"I'm going to take a nap with Mikey," Olivia added.

Crumbling the last of a biscuit onto his plate, the boy let out a howl.

"Hush," his grandmother told him, "or you'll go right now instead of waiting for me."

That quieted his protests. He rubbed the biscuit bits into a tiny pool of sorghum and stuffed the gooey mass into this mouth.

"What needs to be done this afternoon?" Garrett murmured to Liza.

"Olivia has supper mostly taken care of," she said. "There's precious little to do for that. But we should make some goodies for the party tonight and maybe bake some dried-apple pies for tomorrow."

"How about some Poor Man Cookies?" Charlene suggested. "Flour, brown sugar, oatmeal, and a few other things. No eggs. They're simple to make."

"I'll help," Betsy said, glancing hopefully at her mother.

Ginger held her daughter's gaze for a short moment, and Betsy shrank. "We'll do the pies," she told her daughter.

"I'll help you later when I get up from our nap," Olivia told Charlene. Now very familiar with the kitchen, the grandmother found a clean washcloth. Dampening it in a bowl of warm water, she came toward her grandson.

"Show me those patties," she said.

He held up his crumbly, sticky hands for

her to wipe.

"What would we ever do without little boys?" she asked, taking the last bit of biscuit from his cheeks. She bent over and kissed his forehead. "Come to Grandma, honey." She picked him up and carried him to the bedroom, his feet dangling around her knees.

"He's big enough to walk," Garrett said, when the bedroom door closed.

"But there's something special about being carried," Charlene told him. "For the boy and for the grandma."

Ten minutes later, the women finished the dishes and set out for the bunkhouse. Charlene hesitated after Ginger and Betsy left. "I'm tired, and I need to rest," she confided, "but I hate going out there with that old biddy. She cuts me every chance she gets." Pulling the door open, she went out.

"Would you like me to fill your coffee cup again?" Liza asked Garrett.

He nodded. "That would be fine."

Glad he said yes, she took her own cup to the stove as well and ladled them full.

When she returned, he said, "Tell me about your folks, Liza."

She tried to think of where to begin. "They were wonderful parents. The best. They loved each other, and they loved us. I guess that's what really counts."

She absently rubbed the wood grain on the table next to her cup. "We've never been well off, but we've never lacked either. Pa believed in hard work and honest dealings with his neighbors. Ma was up before everyone else and went to bed after we did. She worked her hands raw sometimes."

"Did your father ever think about running anything besides longhorns?" he asked.

She shook her head. "He knew cattle. That's what he always said when anyone mentioned trying farming or logging or breeding horses, or whatever. I don't think he could have done anything else. Bryant's the same way. He's stuck in one groove. I don't think he'll ever do anything else."

"Harvey seems different."

She nodded. "Bryant calls him 'Professor' sometimes. Harvey loves books and learning. He'd like to go to college, but there's not enough money to pay his tuition. So, he saves up and buys books. The loft has a shelf full of them."

Garrett nodded. "I saw them up there. *The Age of Reason* by Thomas Paine, *Principles of Nature* by Elihu Palmer, *Walden* by Thoreau — pretty impressive."

"Expensive, you mean. The philosophies in those books scare me. They don't agree with the Bible at all."

He nodded. "I'm not much of a reader," he said, "but I remember those titles from school."

"I'm afraid that Harvey believes that everything written down in a book must be so. Bryant, on the other hand, thinks the exact opposite. He doesn't trust book learning." She shook her head. "He's too much like Pa, set in his ways and his opinions." She turned to him. "What about your folks? Your mother sounds like a fine person."

He nodded. "She is. She's seen a lot of trouble in her life, though. Since Pa passed away last year, she's had a tough time of it."

"At least she had you," Liza said.

"I don't know why God let me be the one to grow up," he said. "She had three other children, you know. They all died before they reached a year old. Except for me. Sometimes I wonder what the good Lord was thinking when He let that happen."

"I'm glad it was you," she blurted out, then blushed and wished the words back.

He grinned at her. "You know, at this moment, so am I."

Liza's cheeks grew warmer still.

At that instant, the door burst open and Bryant stepped in. When he saw Liza and Garrett so close together at the table, he drew up. His chin lifted.

Not looking at Garrett, he spoke to Liza. "We're heading out for the second run. Last time it took four hours to make the round. I'm expecting to be back around nightfall. If we're not back, wait until morning and send some men after us. The ground's getting slicker by the hour. I'm afraid we may have a horse fall and break a leg."

She stood. "Are you sure you should go?" she asked. "Maybe you should wait a few days, so the ground can dry out."

"We'll try it. If it gets too bad, we'll turn back." Without a good-bye, he ducked out the door.

Liza moved to the door to check that the latch caught. From the look on her older brother's face, she was surely in hot water now. With a small sigh and a little shrug, she returned to the table.

The silence between her and Garrett was taut.

"Garrett," she said, "if the road is as bad as Bryant says, you may not be able to get out if you wait much longer. Are you sure you want to stay?"

"As long as you don't chase me away with a stick," he said.

Chapter 5

They talked until Charlene returned to start the cookies and Olivia came out of the bedroom. Excusing himself, Garrett went out to split some more wood.

Liza moved to the pantry to pull out baking ingredients when Caleb came inside. He looked all in.

"It's a muddy mess out there," he said, sinking into a chair at the table. "The horses have been milling around in the corral churning it up and wearing themselves out. I finally had to put them all in the barn. I wonder how the cows are doing in that canyon, but I'm going to have to wait until tomorrow to find out."

Liza poured him a hot cup of coffee. When any of her brothers came in and sat down, that was a given. "On Christmas Day?" Liza asked. "You've got a few cowboys out there in the barn. Why don't you get a couple of them to go with you this afternoon? Then you can have tomorrow clear."

"What are we doing tomorrow?" he asked.

"A big Christmas dinner," she said. "A holiday celebration, like most folks have. We're planning to eat turkey, dressing, and fill more serving dishes than this table can hold."

"And then some," Olivia agreed. She found a large mixing bowl and brought it to the table. "All right, Charlene," she said, "come and pour out the ingredients for those cookies. I'm going to watch you, so I can make these later."

Caleb finished his coffee about the time that Ginger and Betsy arrived. Tipping his hat to the ladies as they came in, he set off for the barn. A short time later, he rode out with two other men, heading northwest toward the canyon.

Charlene was sliding her first pan of cookies into the oven when a commotion in the yard brought the ladies to the porch. Seven horses were heading through the yard, their steps lagging.

Bryant stopped near the porch. "The creek's flooding the road," he said. "We can't get through. It's too dangerous."

"Caleb and a couple of the men went to check on the canyon," Liza told him. "Could you and Harvey ask the men to set hay bales around and get the barn ready for the party?"

Bryant surveyed the yard. "We've got to do something about this mud," he said. "I think we have some old boards around somewhere. Maybe we can make a boardwalk from the barn to the house, but it's at least a hundred feet. I'm not sure if we can round up that much wood." He shook his head. "All we can do is try."

Rosita brought her mount to the porch stairs and swung down. She handed her reins to Bryant. "Thank you," she said, when he reached for them. "I'll stay here and help the ladies."

"Welcome back!" Charlene said. "We missed you." She turned to Liza. "The party will be more fun with everyone here, at least."

Liza smiled. "You're right, Charlene. It's best to look on the bright side."

Strangely, the party spirit seemed to flow through the cabin as soon as Rosita stepped inside. The younger women told stories and laughed as they baked cookies. Mikey woke up, and Betsy played with him on the carpet while her mother rolled out pie crusts.

Liza tried to blend in with the rest, though her eyes often trailed to the window where Garrett's tall form bent over the chopping block. How long did it take to split a few logs, anyway?

Finally, Garrett came inside for a break and a drink of cool water. He was sitting at the table when Bryant came in. In his stocking feet, he stood by the door to ask Liza, "Are you sure you want to have this party in the barn? The boardwalk sank into the mud. You can't even see it, especially not in the dark."

Liza turned to Charlene. "What do you think?"

"We're going to play Blind Man's Bluff and Musical Chairs," she replied. "There's not enough room in here for them."

Liza nodded then said, "Maybe we should put sawdust on the porch to absorb the mud. At least that'll help keep some of it out of the house." She looked at the splotchy floorboards in the dining room. "I've given up on trying to keep it clean in here, but we can at least try to put a limit on what tracks in."

Garrett stood up. "If you'll show me where the sawdust is, I'll take care of that for you."

Bryant gave him a grudging look. "It's in sacks in the barn. We use it to keep the barn floor dry."

Garrett picked up his hat from a nearby

chair and put it on. He sent Liza a wink an instant before he walked out after her brother.

That evening at supper, Garrett sat across from Liza. In some ways, that was worse than sitting beside him because she couldn't stop looking at him. She tried to pretend that nothing had changed, but her heart was singing too loudly to hide it.

Once she caught Bryant frowning at her, and she lost her breath. He was seriously vexed with her. So seriously that it frightened her.

She found an excuse to get up from the table. Her bowl of beans sat untouched, her cornbread growing dry and hard, but she poured coffee and offered the basket of bread to everyone in the room twice over, ignoring the meal. There would be time for it later. She didn't return to her seat until Bryant had gone out.

When she did, Garrett gave her a sardonic smile. None of the by-play was lost on him. The glint in his eyes told her he knew exactly what had happened.

As usual, Charlene was the first one to set up the dishpan for washing, and Rosita soon joined her. Ginger and Betsy piled cookies into a wide, cloth-lined basket while Olivia took care of a fresh pot of coffee.

As soon as the last dish lay in the cabinet, the group set off in a troop toward the barn. With the cookie basket on Ginger's arm and the cooking pot of hot coffee in Garrett's padded hands, they set off single file. Charlene carried Mikey, so Olivia could hold Rosita's arm with one hand and her black skirts with the other. Liza was last across with a double stack of tin coffee mugs in her hands.

They reached the barn with laughter of relief, congratulating each other on a safe trip. Harvey had found an old dusty table and set it along the wall for the refreshments.

The barn was square-shaped with horse stalls running down two sides, leaving a wide rectangular area open in the center. A dozen hay bales formed a circle along the edges, and the floor held a layer of fresh straw. The area glowed from lanterns hanging on posts all around. Nearby, horses muttered and stamped, mildly irritated at the commotion.

When they'd set out the food and found places to sit, Liza said, "Charlene, you do the honors. You know what's planned."

Charlene turned to Harvey and handed him a scrap of paper. "You call them out," she told him. "I can't stand up in front of all these people."

Liza looked at her, surprised. If Charlene was a dancer, she certainly couldn't be shy.

Harvey headed to the front of the area and called out, "First off, we're going to divide into two teams and play Twenty Questions." He eyed the group and held up his hand with the palm vertical. "We'll divide the room here. Pick your captains and let me know when you're ready." He scanned down the list and glanced at Charlene. "Say, these are pretty good."

Charlene beamed.

Rosita giggled.

They played for an hour, then broke up for cookies and coffee. Garrett picked up several cookies and moved to a seat on the hay bale next to Liza. He offered her one and grinned when she took it. "You're welcome," he said, though she hadn't said thanks.

"You're going to get me into trouble," she said with mock rebuke. "Bryant is watching you. I hope you know it."

"Absolutely," he replied, taking a big bite.

When everyone was seated with food in hand, Olivia said, "How about some testimonies? Has the Lord done anything for you this week? Or maybe this year?"

The cowhands looked uncomfortable.

Harvey, usually the moderator, stayed silent.

Olivia waited a few seconds then went on, "I'm thankful that we're all safe. If the train had been moving just a little faster, we wouldn't be sitting here enjoying this good food and fellowship."

Amens and nods from all directions brought warmth to the room that hadn't been there before.

She continued, "I know that God has His hand in those things. The way I see it, those of us who were on board the train have a special responsibility. God spared our lives. That couldn't have been an accident."

Rosita looked sober.

Charlene looked like she was about to cry.

Garrett cleared his throat. "I wasn't on the train," he said, "but the Lord did bless me last year, and I'd like to tell about it." His voice was mellow, but it carried throughout the room.

"My father had a heart attack last March at the age of forty-three. It was a big shock to Ma and me. He lived for almost a whole day after it happened. The doctor said there was nothing that could be done for him. We knew he wasn't long for this world, and he knew it, too."

He swallowed and rubbed the bridge of

his nose. "I'd just like to say that I'm grateful that God let us have that time with him. We got to sit with him and tell him how much he meant to us. He and Ma had a chance to say their good-byes and promise to meet again on the other side." He paused a moment then went on. "When I miss him, I think about that time, and it helps me feel better."

Glancing around, as though unsure how to end, he said, "That's all."

Liza felt a lump coming into her throat. Her parents had died far away. She and the boys hadn't even seen their bodies. Folks with cholera had to be buried right away and their possessions burned.

In the darkness, she felt Garrett's fingers close around hers, so warm and comforting as though he knew what she was feeling at that moment. She swallowed back her tears and hung on to him.

Finally, Olivia said, "I'd best get to the house. I'm too tired to go on. Mikey's getting cranky, too."

Harvey looked at Liza. "I guess we'd best call it a night," he said. "Thanks, everyone! It was a great time."

Next to Liza, Garrett said, "A wonderful time!"

Liza beamed.

Taking two lanterns, the bunkhouse ladies left first. Those from the cabin tried to pick out the boardwalk under the mud as they made their way across the yard.

Carrying the empty basket, Liza was almost to the porch when her shoes slipped on the slimy board. With a cry, her arms flew up and the basket hit the sludge. Behind her, Garrett's hand shot out to grab her arm. They did a little two-step but managed to keep their balance. Laughing, they made it to the step and climbed to the porch floor.

Liza was about to go inside, when Bryant's arm came across her waist to stop her. Ahead of her, Garrett disappeared through the door, not realizing she wasn't with him.

"I want to talk to you, missy," Bryant said, his eyes hard in the darkness.

Liza gulped and waited, trying to brace herself for what was coming.

"You're making a fool of yourself over that lying Anderson whelp," he said. "I'm warning you, Liza. I'm not taking this."

"Lying?" she demanded. "What makes you say lying? He's never lied to you."

"All Andersons are liars," he retorted. "They have been for generations. You know that as well as I do."

She drew herself up to her full five feet,

two inches. "I do not!"

He bent over with his face close to hers. "I'm not going to argue with you, Liza. I'm *telling* you. You'd better mind what I say."

With that, he took two quick steps and disappeared through the cabin door.

Liza remained on the porch for a few minutes, trying to compose herself before she went inside. She wanted to cry, but she was also furious at Bryant for being so uncaring. She was only a year younger than he was. Why couldn't he trust her judgment enough to give her a chance to tell him what she'd learned about Garrett? It wasn't fair.

On the other hand, her brothers were all she had in the world. Bryant was hotheaded enough to make things really tough on her if she didn't give in to his demands. Were her feelings for Garrett strong enough to warrant such a struggle?

She wasn't sure. She'd never felt for a man like she felt for Garrett. But it could be only a passing thing, the product of unusual circumstances or maybe the phase of the moon. She'd heard that a full moon fostered romance. Or was it the new moon?

She peered out from under the eaves to see what the moon looked like. It was quarter-sized crescent, smiling down at her foolishness.

Shaking her head at her own idiocy, she went inside. The kitchen counters were loaded with a dozen loaves of bread, six pies, crumbled cornbread in a large bowl, and a platter of left-over cookies from that evening's festivities — all covered with dishcloths.

She went to her room, undressed in the darkness, found her way to her edge of the bed, and crept under the heavy eiderdown quilts.

Mikey sighed, a sweet, soft sound.

Although she had to be up at four to make the dressing and put those turkeys in the oven before breakfast, she lay awake long into the night. How could she talk some sense into Bryant? How could she give up Garrett?

Chapter 6

Christmas morning dawned with an icy wind coming from the mountain. It crept in around the windows and under the doors. Garrett was up early, stoking the fires to try to chase away the bone-aching cold. Still, Liza's feet felt like half-frozen stumps as she stuffed both turkeys with cornbread dressing in the pre-dawn. She'd been forced to lay aside her wool shawl for fear of dipping it into the food.

Finally, the birds were in the oven. She was washing her hands when Olivia came out of the bedroom.

"Good morning, Liza," she said. "You know, despite the interruption of our holiday plans, it has been good to see the Wainright cabin again."

"You know this place?" Liza asked, reaching for a hand towel.

"I believe my mother may have worked here when I was a girl," she said, setting the coffeepot under the pitcher pump's spout. "That was more years ago than I care to count." She gave the pump handle four hard, quick pushes. Water gushed out and hit the bottom of the pot with a metallic sound.

Charlene arrived as Olivia was setting the pot on the stove. The younger woman's face was swollen around the eyes, her nose and cheeks red.

"Charlene," Olivia said, concerned. "Are you ill?"

Sniffing, she said, "Only inside, Miss Olivia. I didn't sleep hardly at all last night." She dabbed at her nose and her eyes filled with tears.

Immediately, Olivia went to her. "Honey, what is it?" She drew her to the sofa and sat beside her.

With her ear tuned to their conversation, Liza pulled out the half-empty basket of eggs and started slicing bacon. Garrett moved away from the living room fireplace to join her. They shared a glance but didn't speak.

Charlene's tears grew into soft sobs.

Olivia held her and patted her back. "What is it, child? Did someone say something hurtful to you?"

Charlene shook her head. "It was your

test . . . testimony last night," she quavered. "About God sparing us for a reason." Her breath came in gasps. "I'm so ashamed."

Olivia let her cry for a few moments until she'd settled down a little.

"Charlene, God loves you. He loved you so much that He sent His Son to die for your sins . . . in your place."

Charlene nodded.

She lifted Charlene's chin so she could look into her watery eyes. "Honey, if you had been the only person in the entire world, He would have still died for you."

Tears overflowed onto Charlene's ruddy cheeks. She nodded.

"Tell Him about it," Olivia urged, her voice gentle. "Tell Him how ashamed you are and that you want Him to take away your sin. Let's do it right now."

Again Charlene nodded.

Olivia bowed and Charlene bowed with her so their heads were touching, temple to temple. "Father," Olivia prayed, "your child, Charlene, has come to understand that she needs Your forgiveness. Lord, please hear her and grant her a new life."

When she finished, Charlene said simply, "Lord . . . be merciful to me. I'm a sinner." Her voice broke. "Please take my life and make it new."

They hugged each other with more tears. Liza had tears on her cheeks as well.

With a smile that was just for her, Garrett squeezed her arm then made himself scarce at the woodpile. Liza had seen the same reaction in her brothers. Whenever they saw tears, they wanted to be far away.

Finally, Charlene came to the kitchen.

Liza hugged her hard. "I'm so happy for you," she said. "I wish you were going to stay around here. We've got a good little church in Wiley's Corner. Our pastor is a wonderful man of God. You'd learn a lot from him."

Charlene dipped her hands in the washing-up basin beside the back door and patted her cheeks. "I'm tempted to do that," she said. "I just wish folks hereabout didn't know where I came from."

Olivia said, "It's best to be out front with that instead of trying to hide it away. God's grace is for everyone. If there're people who don't see it that way, then you've lost nothing by not associating with them."

Liza said, "Think of it, Charlene. You received Christ on Christmas morning. What better gift could you ever have?"

"That's right," she said, beaming. "That's right!"

A noise at the door brought them around

to see Rosita step inside. "What's right?" she asked, taking off her wool scarf and smoothing her black hair.

Charlene said, "I received Christ on Christmas morning."

Rosita looked puzzled.

"I'll tell you about it after breakfast," Charlene promised. She washed her hands and dried them. "What's next?" she asked. "Do you want me to make more biscuits?"

"We're eating bread this morning," Liza told her with a grin. "The oven is full of turkey."

The news of Charlene's conversion met with mixed reactions. Liza expected Ginger to be happy for the girl, but she gave no reaction at all. Harvey, surprisingly, seemed enormously pleased.

There were fifteen people at breakfast that Christmas morning: ten passengers, the four Wainrights, and Garrett. After the meal, the men brought the checkerboard to the house, saying that the barn was too cold. A couple of them had found scraps of wood to whittle, and Harvey kept everyone entertained by retelling stories he'd read in Plutarch's *Lives*.

Near noon, Mikey sat at the table with a frown on his dimpled face. "I want my mama," he said, a chant he'd picked up a breakfast and had continued for hours.

Garrett found a seat across from him. Without speaking to the child, he placed his hands together in a prayerful pose then twisted them so that his hands faced each other with a finger wiggling out each side. He held his hands up and examined each wiggling finger as though fascinated.

Mikey stopped whining. He stared at Garrett's hands.

Garrett held them out for Mikey to take a better look, and the boy smacked at them. Tucking his chin down, Mikey grinned.

"Do you want to see how I do it?" Garrett asked, pulling his hands apart.

"I do!" Caleb said, coming away from his position as spectator of the checkers match.

Garrett waited for Caleb to join him at the table. Placing his hands together again, he twisted them.

"Wait!" Caleb said. "I didn't get it."

Garrett spoke to Mikey. "Want me to show him on your hands?" he asked.

Mikey nodded and held out his chubby fingers.

Garrett placed the boy's palms together, pushed down one finger from each hand and twisted the palms.

Mikey let out a delighted squeal as he wiggled his displaced fingers. "Look,

Grandma!" he cried.

Olivia laughed. "My brothers used to do that one," she said. "I haven't seen it for years."

Caleb tried to imitate Garrett's moves but failed. Finally, Garrett pressed the boy's hands into the right position.

"I got it!" he said, separating them and fitting them together again.

Setting a pot of potatoes on to boil, Liza chuckled. "Where did you get that from?" she asked.

"Our old foreman," Garrett told her. "He knew all kinds of tricks, and he kept me entertained when I was this age." He ruffled Mikey's straw-colored hair.

Careful to keep his hands together, Mikey eased out of his chair and made the circuit around the room to show his fingers to each adult in turn. Halfway around, he tripped and his hands came apart. Running to Garrett, he said, "Do them again!"

"Please," Olivia told him.

"Please," he said, his former pout totally forgotten. When Garrett had him set, he ran back to the last cowboy, then moved into the kitchen to show the ladies.

"That was good of you," Olivia told Garrett.

He stood and reached for a stick of wood

in the box beside the stove. "I'm glad it worked," he said, grinning at the happy child.

That Christmas dinner was the biggest meal Liza had ever overseen. There were so many serving dishes that they had to set up a side table just for the food. Turkey and dressing, mashed potatoes, sweet potatoes, pickles in several forms, corn, cabbage salad, boiled greens, fresh rolls, and plenty of pies. By one o'clock, everyone had eaten his or her fill, and there was still food to spare.

Clearing away the leftovers, Liza remarked to Olivia, "Before the avalanche, we had barely enough food to last the winter. Now look at all this food just a couple of days later. I feel like the four starving lepers while Samaria was under siege. The prophet promised that by tomorrow this time there would be more food than they all could eat."

Olivia said, "I know that story. One of the king's men said, 'If God opened the windows of heaven, could this be?' "

Liza nodded. "Then the lepers went out to the enemy camp and found more to eat than they could carry away."

Olivia smiled. "In your case, the food came in on horseback."

"And wagonload," Garrett added.

Carrying plates to the dishpan, Charlene was listening intently. "Where is that story in the Bible?" she asked. "I'd like to read it sometime."

"I think it's in the Kings," Olivia told her. "We'll look it up later. I have a Bible in my case."

Rosita carried the old dishwater out the back door to pitch it onto the ground. When she returned, she said, "What are we going to do with the rest of the day?"

Ginger stretched her back. "I'm going to take a rest. We'll likely be heading home tomorrow, and the washing pile that will be waiting for me will be a sight to behold. I guarantee it."

"Do you think we'll be able to leave tomorrow?" Rosita asked.

Bryant answered from across the room. "I rode out to check the stream after breakfast. It's going down. As long as we don't get any more rain, we may be able to cross it in the morning. No promises, though." He again focused on the checkerboard.

Charlene looked troubled, but she stayed busy with drying the dishes and didn't say anything.

Olivia said, "I've got to have a couple of days at home. Then we'll take a stage to the next open rail station so Mikey can get home to his mother. She's frantic to see him, I know."

"I'll hate to see you go," Liza said. She turned to include those in the kitchen. "All of you. I know that this has been a problem for you all, but you've been a blessing to me."

"You're sweet to say that," Olivia said. "I hope this won't be good-bye forever. Canton's Corner isn't so far away. Please come and see me sometime."

One by one, folks wandered off to their own places, leaving Bryant and Joshua intent on a checkers game and a couple of cowboys dozing in chairs beside the fire. Olivia took Mikey for a nap, and the house grew quiet.

"How about a walk?" Garrett asked Liza, speaking softly so no one else could hear.

"In this cold?" she whispered back.

"We could find someplace out of the wind, I reckon."

"I'll get an extra sweater," she said and tiptoed into the bedroom to find one. In a moment, she returned.

Bundling into coats, scarves, and hats, they left the house by the back way and eased the door closed behind them.

"Where to?" he asked, when they were in the yard.

"Let's go around the mud in the yard and get behind the barn. There's a high fence on that side of the corral that would give some shelter."

The wind snatched the breath from their lungs. It crept down their collars and up their coat sleeves. By the time they reached the corral, Liza was shivering.

"We won't be able to stay long," she said. "We shouldn't anyway. Bryant will be missing me before long."

Shoving his hands deep into his coat pockets, Garrett said, "Is tomorrow going to be good-bye for us, too?"

She hesitated. With all her heart she wanted to say no, but she wasn't sure. "What should I do? Bryant won't listen to me. He's got his mind made up, and nothing will change it. I know that just as sure as I know I'm standing here."

"Why does that have to affect us?" he asked. "Aren't you an adult now? Can't you make up your own mind?"

"My brothers are all I have," she said. "They're Wainrights, all three of them. I can't forget that I'm one, too."

He leaned back and looked straight up at the blue sky. "Why did our grandfathers do this to us?" he asked. He looked at her once more. "No one knows how the bad feelings started, so how can we make an end of it?" He peered at her. "What do you know about the feud, Liza? What was the story that came down through your family?"

"That the Andersons are liars and cheats," she said.

He bristled.

She tugged at the middle button on his coat. "You asked me. That's what I heard. That's what the boys have heard. That's all I know."

"Nothing else?" he asked. "Surely there must have been something more, some reason for such a reputation."

She shook her head. "My father only spoke of it once or twice that I remember. And that's all he said."

Turning sideways to her, he leaned against the fence. "I hope you'll believe me when I say that my father was an honest, God-fearing man. So was his father before him. They were men of faith who prayed and read the Bible to their families every morning of their lives."

Liza stared at him. She could hardly believe what she was hearing. Why had her grandfather been so adamant that the Andersons were wicked? She said, "What did you hear about us?"

He drew in a breath before answering. "I

hope you're ready to hear this," he said. "Remember, it's what I was told, not what I personally think about you." He caught her hand and held it. "I was told that the Wainrights are malicious liars, that they set out to destroy people for no reason."

Liza said, "My father scorned religion of any kind and so did my grandfather. But I've never known either one of them to tell a lie, Garrett. A man's word is his bond. You know that. That's what they lived by." Her eyes narrowed. "If either of our grandfathers had been dishonest, they would have never been able to do business with anyone in these parts."

"But both of them were respected in their own right," he said.

"The only people who had misgivings about them were each other." She looked at him. "Does your mother know anything?" she asked. "Maybe you should ask her for more information."

"As soon as I get home, that's exactly what I'll do," he said. "I've got good reason to find where this all started." He hesitated, watching her closely. "At least I hope I do."

"Garrett . . ."

"I know I may be rushing things," he said, interrupting her. "But the fact is, I don't know when I'll have another chance to talk to you. Your brothers may run me off with a shotgun if I come back later."

She wanted to deny it, but she knew what he said was true.

Standing, he looked into her eyes and went on. "You've been special to me since we were kids in Miss Casey's school. When Ma suggested that I bring over food and supplies, I agreed to it because I'd have a chance to see you again." He searched her face. "I love you, Liza. Is there any hope for me?"

"Garrett . . ."

He put his gloved hand over her mouth. "Don't tell me what Bryant wants you to say. Speak what's in your own heart. Please." He removed his hand to let her speak.

The anguish on his face tore at her heart. "I love you, too," she said simply. "But I . . ."

She didn't get any further. Drawing her close, he leaned down and kissed her until her head was spinning.

She'd never felt so sheltered as she did at that moment.

"We've got to fight," he said, whispering into her hair. "We can't let a fifty-year-old argument keep us apart."

She nodded, her rounded cheek brushing the front of his black coat. "I want to," she said, "but how?"

He drew back enough to look into her face. "I'll talk to my mother. Maybe she can remember something that will give us a place to start."

"But what if finding the reason doesn't make any difference? What if Bryant won't listen?"

"If Grandfather Anderson was wrong, I'll make restitution if it takes giving up my entire ranch," he said. "No one could argue with that. If Grandfather Wainright was wrong, then at least the Andersons can have a chance to forgive him." Garrett's voice had new steel in it. His arms tightened. "I'm not going to lose you now that we've found each other."

He kissed her again.

Breathless, Liza pulled away. "We've got to go back inside. Bryant will come looking for us, and then I'll really be in trouble."

"You're right," he said, kissing her cheek. "If I go home tomorrow, I'll meet you right here at dusk two days from now."

She nodded. "I'll be waiting for you."

Chapter 7

Peering around the corner to be sure the way was clear, hand in hand they hustled around the yard. Releasing her, Garrett headed for the woodpile to gather wood.

Liza paused outside the back door to calm her breathing and then returned to the warmth of the house. She quickly shrugged out of her coat and eased open the bedroom door to lay her wraps inside. Olivia and Mikey lay sleeping quietly under the nine-square quilt.

To stay out of Bryant's range of sight, Liza busied herself with sweeping the dining room floor near the back door.

Garrett came in and dropped a dozen split logs into the wood box next to the kitchen stove. "It's bitter out there," he remarked, his tone casual.

"Would you like some coffee?" Liza asked. "There's still a little left."

"Bring us some, too," Bryant called from

the living room.

When Liza brought her brother his coffee, he muttered, "Where have you been?"

She felt her face flush. "Out for some air," she said, avoiding his eyes.

Bryant didn't speak again. His harsh stare told her all she needed to know.

A few minutes later, she joined Garrett at the table. "He's on to us," she whispered.

Under the table, he squeezed her hand. "It's going to be all right," he murmured. "I promise you that."

Her chin lifted. "I'm tired of being Bryant's bondslave," she retorted, still whispering.

The door opened and Charlene stepped inside, her blond hair blowing across her face. She pushed the door shut and tried to smooth it back, but several wisps hung about her face, giving her an ethereal look.

Shrugging out of her cape, she came to join Garrett and Liza. Harvey came in behind her and moved to the living room without saying anything to those in the kitchen.

Watching the other girl's downcast face, Liza asked, "What's the problem?"

Charlene shrugged. "I don't know where to go," she replied. "I can't go back to my old job. My parents have . . . That is, they don't want me to come home." She looked down at her hands. "When we leave tomorrow, what should I do?"

The bedroom door clicked shut. "Come home with me," Olivia said, stepping to the table. "I've got a spare room, and my house will be mighty quiet once Mikey goes home." She placed her hand on Charlene's shoulder. "God will make a way for you, my dear. He's already begun."

Charlene nodded, fighting tears. "You're a saint, Miss Olivia," she whispered.

The older woman shook her head. "No, Charlene. I'm a sinner . . . reborn by the grace of God. The same as you."

Leaving Charlene, Olivia turned toward the kitchen. "What shall we do to feed those hungry mouths this evening?" she asked. "It's almost five o'clock. We're going to start hearing from the crowd pretty soon."

"Let's just set out leftovers," Liza said, getting up from her seat. "I set some bowls out into cold storage. I'll get them." She rushed outside without stopping for her coat, Charlene right behind her.

Returning in less than a minute, both girls gasped as they shut the door behind them, their hands full of dishes.

Garrett was piling still more wood into the kitchen stove.

Olivia came to relieve them of their burdens. "What were you thinking?" she gasped, shivering. "You should have taken your wraps out there. I'm getting a chill from standing next to you."

She poured food into pans and set them to warm while Liza made more coffee. Charlene began setting up the dishpan for the after-dinner cleanup.

Harvey moved to the kitchen table. Leaning back, he stretched his legs straight out. "Say, Charlene," he said. "How about another game of Twenty Questions this evening? Do you think you can come up with some more good ideas?"

She turned, surprised. "I suppose I could," she said hesitantly.

He turned to Liza. "Sis, find us a piece of paper. We can plan it out now." He looked at Charlene. "Ten things would be enough, don't you think?"

"That should be plenty," she said, moving to sit across from him. "But we can't stay up late tonight again."

He nodded. "We'll be leaving before daybreak, if I know Bryant."

A *harrumph* sounded from the living room. "Six o'clock," his older brother called.

Harvey went on. "You'll have to sit here, Charlene." He pulled out the chair next to him. "Otherwise, everyone will hear what we're saying."

Liza looked up and caught Garrett watching her, an amused expression on his face. When he sent a pointed glance toward the couple at the table, Liza's eyes widened. She looked at Garrett and he winked, then leaned down to check the fire in the cook stove.

When the passengers had gone to their quarters, Harvey lingered in the living room watching Bryant put away the checker pieces. Harvey glanced at his sister in the kitchen and directed his question to her. "You could use some help around here, right?"

She nodded. "Who couldn't," she asked, wiping the counter and wondering where he was going with this.

He looked at Bryant. "How would you feel about Charlene staying on and helping Liza around here?" he asked. "She has no place to go."

Bryant considered. "Olivia offered her a place, Harvey. Why do you want her to stay on here?"

Harvey's sensitive mouth tightened. "I'd like her to stay, that's all."

"Are you sure that's wise?" Liza asked. "You've only just met. Why don't you ride to Canton's Corner every couple of weeks to see her instead?" She glanced at Bryant. "I think she'd benefit from being with Olivia for a while. They are good friends, and Olivia would be a good influence on her. Charlene needs that now."

Bryant nodded. "There is some sense to what Liza says, Harv."

"But Canton's Corner is half a day's ride," Harvey protested. "How about if we give Charlene the option and let her make up her own mind?"

Liza had a sinking feeling. Harvey wasn't a Christian. With all that twisted philosophy he read, he wouldn't be a good influence on Charlene.

Listening from the dining room where the brothers couldn't see him, Garrett gave Liza a nod. She went on. "Let's sleep on it," she told the boys. "We'll talk to Charlene before breakfast. She always comes early to help with the cooking."

With no more work to do, Liza had no excuse to stay up later. Bryant seemed determined to wait up until Garrett also retired, so she said good night and went to bed. Garrett had wanted to say something to her, but she hadn't had a chance to find out what it was.

Sometime during the night, a tapping on

her window brought her awake. Frightened at first, she finally woke up enough to realize that it might be Garrett. She slipped into the hard leather of her frigid shoes and found her coat in the dark, still lying where she'd thrown it yesterday afternoon.

She crept out to the back porch, and Garrett's lanky form appeared from the shadow of the cold storage wall.

"What is it?" she asked, shivering.

He drew Liza into his arms and quickly whispered, "Talk to Charlene and tell her that my mother would pay her forty dollars a month to help with the cooking and cleaning."

"But what about Harvey? He's got his eye on that girl, Garrett, and he's not a good influence on her."

He let out a mirthless chuckle. "Do you think Harvey would come to the Anderson ranch for any reason? Do you really?"

She sighed. "I see your point. Okay. I'll speak to her in the morning." She pulled away. "My feet are numb. I've got to get back inside."

He let her go. "I've got to figure out how to get back up that ladder without waking the crew."

She reached up to kiss his cheek. "Thanks for caring about Charlene," she said. "Just be careful you don't start caring too much!" He grabbed her back to him and kissed her. "No danger of that." He kissed her again.

Giggling, she freed herself and hurried back inside.

Despite her soft bed and warm blankets, she didn't sleep much for the rest of the night. Tomorrow everything would change. She dreaded seeing how much.

Out of bed and dressed long before the others awoke, Liza stoked the fires and put on the pot for coffee. She prayed that Charlene would wake up early enough to give them a chance to speak privately.

A few minutes later, the young woman arrived. "I couldn't sleep," she said, "and I figured I may as well come over and start breakfast."

Liza hugged her and urged her toward a chair at the dining room table. "I've been up praying that you'd come," she said. "I've got to talk to you."

Keeping her voice very low, she outlined the three choices that lay before Charlene without mentioning Harvey. "I'd love to have you here," she said, "but I'm not sure how wise that is at this point."

"What do you think I should do?" Charlene asked.

"As much as I love Olivia," Liza replied, "I think the Anderson ranch is your best bet. What if you can't find work in Canton's Corner? Olivia can't afford to keep you for long herself. From what Garrett says, his mother needs help."

Charlene nodded. "I'll do that, then."

"She's a Christian woman," Liza said. "They go to our church, so I'll see you there every week."

Charlene brightened. "Say, that's all right."

"You can go with Garrett this morning. I think he's leaving before breakfast."

"Before? I've got to get ready."

Liza smiled. "Go ahead. I'll make the biscuits this morning."

The breakfast crowd seemed small with Garrett and Charlene already gone.

"Where's Charlene?" Harvey asked Liza, coming close beside her at the stove to speak privately.

"She had a job offer. She left an hour ago," Liza replied. "She's going to be a housemaid and cook at the Anderson ranch. Mrs. Anderson needs help, from what I understand."

"You're kidding! Why that . . ."

Liza's chin lifted. "That what?"

Clamping his mouth tight, Harvey picked up his hat and headed outside. A few minutes later, he came out of the barn on horseback and trotted toward the canyon.

Before the sun peeked over the mountaintop, the remaining women were exchanging hugs and saying good-byes. With promises of letters, they boarded the wagon and tied their bonnets more tightly against the fitful wind. Mikey laid his head on his grandmother's lap, and she covered him with a rug.

When the wagon lurched forward, Olivia waved at Liza. "God bless you, my dear," she called.

Liza remained on the porch until the last cowboy disappeared from sight. Caleb had gone with Bryant, as usual, so she was the only one left on the place. It seemed like a graveyard after all the excitement of the past three days.

She stepped inside and closed the door. Leaning against it, she looked over the cabin. It seemed different to her.

Pulling off her coat, she rolled up her sleeves and set about clearing away the breakfast dishes. The boys would be starving when they returned. She had to get bread started and decide what to make for dinner. In spite of the massive meals they'd prepared for the stranded passengers, the pantry still seemed overloaded.

"Though I open the windows of heaven..."

Waiting two days to speak again with Garrett seemed just a few minutes short of an eternity. Liza scrubbed the mud-caked floorboards. She washed her neglected laundry and cooked six meals. The whole time she seemed to have one eye on the wind-up clock on the mantel shelf, wishing away the hours. It was exhausting work.

Finally, the sun sank below the horizon on the evening of the second day. She bundled into her coat and two scarves and hurried toward the corral.

When she arrived, Garrett was waiting.

She fell into his arms.

"I've missed you something fierce," he murmured into her hair.

"Not as much as I've missed you," she declared.

"I've got so much to tell you," he said, keeping her close. "Charlene sends her love, by the way, and her thanks. She and Mother are getting along famously."

"I'm so glad." She drew away from him. "What did you find out?"

"Mother doesn't know many details about

the original argument, but she said that I should pay a visit to my father's maiden sister, Johanna, who lives in Canton's Corner."

"I want to come," she said.

His brow creased as though he were wondering if she'd lost her mind. "Is that possible? How could you get away?"

"I'll tell Bryant I'm going to visit Olivia," she said. "And I will."

"Are you sure? Who would cook for the boys while you're away?"

"Harvey is a pretty good hand in the kitchen. I'll make some extra things and leave them in cold storage. How long would it take to get there and come back?"

"One full day, I reckon. If we leave early enough, we could be back by nightfall."

She nodded. "That settles it. I'm going. They'll hardly miss me."

He looked concerned. "You'd have to spend the whole day in the saddle. Are you up to that?"

"You haven't had a chance to know that about me yet, Garrett," she said with a daring look in her eye. "Horses are my passion. I can ride most men out of the saddle."

He suddenly grinned. "You don't say!" He leaned down to kiss her. "You're getting better and better all the time." He moved to kiss her again.

She pulled back. "We've got to make plans. When are you planning to leave?"

"Before daybreak in the morning."

She nodded. "I'll meet you by the lightning-struck oak tree." Stepping away from him, she peeked around the corner. "The boys are still in the canyon, but I'm expecting them back any moment. You'd better ride while you have a chance."

He grabbed her hand and pulled her back into his arms. "Not without a proper goodbye."

Chapter 8

The next morning, the rising sun found Garrett and Liza more than halfway to Canton's Corner. North and east of their ranches, the small town lay on the Colorado plain. Once the riders came out of the foothills, they made good progress.

Liza rode Sassy, her favorite bay mare, named for her spirit and staying power. Wearing jeans with a full skirt over them, she had an easy posture in the saddle and a gentle hand on the reins.

On a feisty black, Garrett sat a full two hands higher than Liza. With his added height, he made her feel like a child riding next to him.

When they stopped to let the horses rest and drink from a small spring, they sat next to each other on a flat rock. Liza pulled out a packet of biscuits and fried ham.

"Do you think your aunt will know anything about the argument between Jacob and Ryan?" she asked.

He munched and swallowed. "It's hard to tell. I'm amazed at how little the older generation talked about their family's history."

"Maybe it was too painful," Liza said, lifting her canteen for a long drink. She screwed on the metal cap. "If we get there early enough, we can spend an hour or so with Olivia. I'd like that."

"Let's go," he said. Standing, he gave her his hand and pulled her to her feet.

They arrived in Canton's Corner just after ten o'clock and found Johanna Anderson's cottage a few minutes later. She lived in a tiny cabin near the church's graveyard. It had a small yard with window boxes at both front windows.

"Why, Garrett!" she exclaimed, opening the front door to his knock. A tall, husky woman, Johanna Anderson was almost the same size as her nephew. The family resemblance was striking, from the dark curly hair to the strong jaw.

"Come in!" She stepped back to let them enter.

"This is Liza Wainright," Garrett said, his arm about Liza's shoulders.

"Nice to meet you, Miss Anderson," Liza said, suddenly nervous under the older woman's scrutiny.

"Nice to meet you, too," she replied, a touch of irony in her voice. "Won't you come in? Would you like some tea?"

When they said they would, she left them in the sitting room to put on the teakettle. Garrett found a spot on the sofa. An ornately carved piece, it must have come from New York or Paris.

Liza hesitated until he patted the place beside him. "Don't go weak-kneed on me now," he teased her. When she sat down, he went on, more seriously, "Aunt Johanna is a straight shooter. She'll help us if she can."

The lady in question appeared at that moment and took a seat in the matching chair nearby. "What can I do for you, Garrett?" she asked. "I have a feeling you had a definite purpose in coming here."

Garrett relaxed on the sofa and said, "Aunt Johanna, what can you tell us about the disagreement between your father and the Wainrights? Do you know what caused the bad blood between our families?"

She glanced from Liza to him. "Papa was very bitter about it, and he wouldn't speak of it. He wouldn't let your father or me mention the name Wainright in passing when we were talking of schoolmates or anything else."

The teakettle whistled, and she hurried to make their tea. In a few minutes, she returned with a small porcelain pot and three china cups on matching saucers.

"However, my mother told me the story . . . as much as she knew of it," she went on as though uninterrupted. Serving the tea, she said, "My father, Ryan Anderson, was the foster son of Matthew Wainright. Ryan was the son of Wainright's partner and good friend. When his parents both died of cholera, Matthew took Ryan in at the age of twelve and treated him as his own son."

She paused to sip. "Matthew had a son of his own who was a year older than Ryan. That was Liza's grandfather, Jacob Wainright. The boys didn't get along. That was the root cause of all this evil. Jacob resented Ryan's coming into the family. Ryan was jealous of Jacob's standing as the natural-born son of Matthew."

"This is getting a little confusing," Garrett said. "Would you mind if I write some of it down so I can keep it straight in my mind?"

She set down her cup. "Of course. I have some writing paper in the secretary." She moved to a small desk with an inlaid design in the fold-up cover and found a single page. Picking up a pencil, she brought them to him with a book to rest them on.

Garrett wrote quickly. "So the two boys, Ryan and Jacob, didn't like each other." He glanced at Liza. "They were our grandfathers."

Johanna nodded. "They each had one son. Jacob's son was . . ."

"Luke Wainright," Liza said when Johanna hesitated. "My father."

The older woman nodded.

Still writing, Garrett said, "Ryan's son was Robert, who was my father."

"Back to the story," Johanna went on. "When Ryan was eighteen, the trouble started. One of the only things that Ryan had left from his parents was a small locket that had belonged to his mother. He treasured the locket and kept it close to his bedside in a drawer. One day it came up missing. He accused Jacob of stealing it, just to spite him. Jacob denied it, but the locket was never found. From the way the story goes, they never spoke to each other again."

She shrugged. "That's not much to go on, I know. But that's what my mother told me. Two years later, Matthew was killed by a bull. The boys split up the ranch with a long stretch of wire, and you know the rest."

Liza was disappointed. She wasn't sure

what she'd hoped to hear, but it wasn't something this intangible. Had Jacob stolen the locket for pure meanness? She thought of Bryant and his sometimes-spiteful ways. Was Jacob like that?

Johanna finished her tea. "Would you like some more?" she asked. When they refused, she set her cup on the tray. "I never could figure out why my father didn't sell his half of the ranch and go somewhere else. Why did he stay right there, neighbors with the Wainrights for the rest of his life? If it had been me, I'd have moved to Texas. What's worse, my father didn't like cattle. He didn't love horses either."

She looked at Garrett. "How is your mother?" she asked. "I haven't had a letter from her in more than a month."

They chatted of family news then Garrett told her of the avalanche and his stay at the Running W. Finally, they stood to go.

"We've got another visit to make before we move on," he said. "We need to be back tonight."

Johanna saw them to the door and kissed her nephew's cheek. "You are so like your father," she said. "I still miss him terribly."

He hugged her. "So do we." When he let her go, he said, "Liza lost both her parents a few years ago. Cholera."

"My dear," Johanna said, "I'm so sorry!"

They talked a few more minutes, then said their final good-byes. As Garrett and Liza returned to their horses, Liza said, "She's a fine person."

Garrett smiled sadly. "Mother asked her to come and stay with us, but she loves her little house and doesn't want to leave it. I only wished she lived closer."

Back in the saddle, they wound their way through Canton's Corner and finally stopped in front of a clapboard structure on the main street near the local school.

"I hope this is the right place," Liza said, swinging down.

"If it's not, we can ask here. Surely most folks around would know Olivia."

But the lady herself answered the door. She gasped and then laughed. "Well, you took me at my word, I see," she said, reaching for Liza's arm. "Come in out of the cold, child. I'm so glad you've come."

"Mr. Garrett!" Mikey's shrill voice came from inside. He ran to Garrett and clasped him about the knees.

Laughing, Garrett lifted the boy and gave him a hug. "Hello, old man. I bet you didn't expect to see us so soon."

"Let's go in here," Olivia said, fitting a key into the first door to the right. "I keep it locked when my company is less than ten years old."

The cold inside hit them with a force when they entered. "Garrett," Olivia said, "would you light the fire? There's kindling already laid in the firebox and some matches in a tin on the shelf."

He found the matches and knelt to light the wood.

It was a room the size of Liza's sitting room and furnished with two padded rockers, a short, plush-covered sofa with dark wood trim, and several small tables. Liza chose one rocking chair, Olivia the other to catch the first warm rays from the fire. When the blaze rose higher, Garrett sat on the sofa with Mikey on his lap.

Liza said, "We came to Canton's Corner to visit Garrett's aunt. We couldn't be so close to you and leave town without stopping to see you."

Olivia looked puzzled. "I barely got home before you arrived. You must have come here for a special reason."

Watching Mikey play the finger game, Garrett replied, "We came to ask Aunt Johanna what she knows about the feud between our families."

Liza added, "We're on a quest to find out why our grandfathers hated each other.

They were foster brothers, you know."

Olivia nodded. "I know. The missing locket."

Sitting bolt upright, Liza gasped. "You know about it? Why didn't you tell me?"

She looked slightly offended. "It wasn't my place, child. I didn't want to put my nose where it didn't belong." She glanced at Garrett. "Besides, I wasn't fully sure how matters stood between the two of you until now."

"Bryant has forbidden me to see Garrett," Liza said. "If only we could put this feud to rest." She leaned forward, urgency in her voice. "Can you tell us what you know about the locket?"

Olivia watched her intent expression. "Why is it so important? What can be changed after so many years?"

Garrett replied, "I'm determined to do what I can to make amends. If Jacob was falsely accused, I want to make that public. If he was guilty, I want to forgive him posthumously. Whatever it takes to put this animosity to rest."

"If that's possible," Liza added ruefully. "Bryant is very bitter about an argument he knows little about. But that doesn't mean he'll be quick to change his mind. He never is."

The older woman nodded and pursed her lips. "Fifty years ago my mother was hired help to Priscilla Wainright, Matthew's poor wife. When the incident with the locket happened, my mother was at their home to help with holiday cooking because Priscilla had been ill." She thought back for a moment. "It was a few months before I turned sixteen. That would make it Christmas of 1833."

She absently rocked for a few seconds. "My mother came home very upset that day. She liked Priscilla, felt sorry for her in a way, I guess."

"Why was that?" Liza asked.

"Matthew could be difficult. He had a way of making up his mind in a snap judgment, and nothing could dissuade him, least of all his wife."

Liza nodded.

"Well, the boys, Ryan and Jacob, ended up enemies from that horrible day onward. Priscilla was heartbroken to have such a rift within their family. She and Matthew loved Ryan as much as if he'd been their own son."

Suddenly, Mikey struggled to get down from the sofa. "I'll get my soldier!" he cried and ran from the room. His shoes thumped loudly on the hallway floor.

Garrett asked Olivia, "Is there any way that we could find out whether Jacob really took the locket? Did it ever come to light again? If he had taken it, what did he do with it?"

"He could have thrown it into the creek," Liza said, "but what good would that have done him? I think it would have been better for him to drop it somewhere where it could be found and clear his name. Then the unpleasantness would have disappeared. I just can't believe that he would have been so callous toward his mother, if she was that upset about it."

"I can't either," Olivia agreed. "When he saw what a stir followed, he would have given it back somehow. From what I knew of those boys, neither of them was that mean spirited."

"You knew them?" Lisa gasped.

"Of course I did, child. Ryan came to call on me a few times." She smiled at Garrett. "I thought of him when I first saw you. You are very like him. He was a kind man, a devoted Christian."

"As my father was," Garrett said, leaning forward to prop his elbows on his knees and clasp his hands. He looked at Liza as though to confirm what he'd already told her about his family.

"Did he sell it and regret it later?" Liza asked.

Olivia said, "That time of year folks stayed at home. Anyone leaving the ranch in winter weather would have been examined for insanity. I doubt that Jacob left the area."

"What else could have happened to the locket?" Liza asked.

Olivia sighed. "That's the big question. But how to answer it after all these years?" Her expression suddenly changed. "Wait a minute." She closed her hazel eyes in an expression that told she was thinking hard. "Mother told me that Priscilla was quite a writer. She spent hours writing letters and recording things that happened with Matthew's business. She must have had a special friend or a relative that she wrote to. Those letters could shed some light on what happened that day."

Liza clapped her hands. "What a brilliant idea! If she wrote to someone, that person would have written back to her. If we find out who wrote to Priscilla regularly, we may be able to track him or her down and find Priscilla's old letters. They're probably in a box in some dusty attic." She turned to Garrett. "We've got a storage room at one end of the loft. There's where we'll find them, if they're still around."

He said, "That's right. Ryan and Jacob slept in the same loft where your brothers sleep now, didn't they?"

Olivia nodded. "It's the same cabin where my mother worked. I lived in Wiley's Crossing until I married Mr. O'Bannon the following year."

They talked a few minutes more then the young people rose to leave. "We have to be back home by nightfall," Liza said. "It isn't fitting for us to be out alone after dark."

Olivia hugged her. "I'm so glad you came to me. Please come again before too long." She saw them to the door. "My prayers go with you," she said before she closed it after them.

They got back in the saddle. Before they set off, Liza said, "I hate to mention this, but I'm starving."

Garrett laughed. "So am I. Let's see what we can find to eat while we ride. That sun is moving way too fast for my liking."

Half an hour later, they each carried a fat sandwich wrapped in paper. They cantered until the town had disappeared behind them, then slowed to eat the food and talk.

"What did Bryant say when you told him you were coming with me?" Garrett asked, reaching for his canteen.

"I didn't tell him," Liza replied, keeping

her face turned downward. "I left a note on the table with breakfast. There was a pot of beans on the back of the stove for their lunch and supper meals."

Garrett gulped a mouthful of water. "You didn't tell him?"

"He wouldn't have let me go. I know he wouldn't."

"Right. But what's he going to do when you get back?"

She shrugged. "I guess I'll find out when I get there, won't I?"

"Liza, I hate to see you in trouble because of me."

She sent him a wry look. "It's a little late to think of that, isn't it?"

He grew quiet, and they finished their lunch. Stuffing the empty paper into his saddlebag, Garrett urged his horse close to her so that their legs brushed.

"I'm going back with you to face him," he said, his jaw set.

"What? Do you want to get shot?" she asked, horrified.

"I'm not going to hide around corners anymore. Bryant is the one who's wrong. Why should we be acting guilty?"

"I have to live with him, though," she said, weakly.

"Maybe not. We'll see about that." He

leaned over to kiss her on the cheek. "Bryant's not the only one who can make up his mind, my love. I'm not going to have you taking the pounding for both of us."

She looked into his deep brown eyes. "One part of me wishes you could just take me away from there."

He reached for her hand and kissed it. "One of these days, I will do just that."

But I love my brothers, too, Liza thought as they picked up the pace again. What was she going to do?

Chapter 9

They reached the Running W on the edge of dark. Leaving Garrett's black horse tied on the edge of the property, they led Sassy into the barn. The yard was still spongy, but not soupy as it had been before.

When they walked into the barn, Caleb was inside tending the stock.

He strode to Liza, his face an angry mask. "You've bought yourself a peck of trouble, Liza," he ground out. "Going off with that no-account . . ."

Her chin came up. "His name is Garrett, and you will call him that."

Her little brother backed down a fraction. "Bryant is furious. He's in the cabin waiting for you." He grabbed the horse's reins. "I'll take care of Sassy. You'd best get to the house." He turned his back on her and led the horse further inside.

Liza's stomach churned. For a second she thought she might be sick. The last thing on earth she wanted to do was face Bryant with him in a temper.

Garrett slipped his arm about her waist. "I'm here, Liza. If it gets too bad, I'll take you home. One way or the other, meet me at that same tree in two days at sundown. Can you do that?"

She nodded, then turned to face him. "At first I didn't want you to come here tonight, but now I'm so glad you did."

He touched her chin. "Can you trust me to take care of this?"

She nodded.

"Let's go fight a lion," he said, winking.

They strode to the cabin, up the porch steps, and through the front door.

Bryant had a single lamp lit. It was in the center of the dining room table. He rose from his chair when they came in, his face eerie from the lamp's yellow glow beneath him. He didn't speak, just stood and stared at them.

Leaving Liza at the door, Garrett strode to him. "Bryant, I want to make peace between us," he said. "You have my apologies for all the childish fighting in the school yard. I shouldn't have taken on my father's grudges. It was wrong."

Bryant still didn't speak. The corner of his mouth twitched.

Garrett went on. "I'm in love with your sister. I want to court her, Bryant. I'm asking you all right and proper for your blessing."

"That's something you'll never get," Bryant snarled. "I ought to get my Sharps .56 and run you outta here."

Liza came to stand beside Garrett. "That wouldn't do any good. Asking your blessing is a sop, Bryant. I'm going to see Garrett one way or the other. I'm a grown woman, and I can make my own choices."

"Not and live in this house, you can't," he said, focusing his blistering stare at her.

At that point, Harvey came down the loft stairs. He stood near Liza, his eyes on his older brother. "That's not the way I see it," Harvey said, his voice calm. "Liza has every right to choose her own man. Just like you and I have a right to choose our own wives."

Bryant's expression turned to disbelief. "You and I will hash this out later," he threatened.

Harvey straightened to his full height. "I'm not afraid of you, Bryant. You can whip me, sure, but you can't change my mind. I'm not ten years old anymore."

Bryant turned his attention back to Garrett. "If Liza's fool enough to want you, she can have you, but only off this property. If you come back on my land again, I'll shoot you. Brother-in-law or not."

Garrett reached for Liza's hand. "As you wish," he said. He glanced at Harvey, a flicker of thanks in his eyes, but didn't speak. Giving Liza's hand a quick squeeze, he headed for the door and walked out.

Liza stood stock still beside her bedroom door. One part of her was afraid of Bryant's anger, but another part was furious. Who did he think he was, ordering her around like a child?

The tension in the room was taut as a banjo string. Glaring at each other, Bryant and Harvey seemed to have forgotten her.

"So, you're taking the bit in your teeth?" Bryant ground out. "I may just kick you out, too."

"Oh yeah," Harvey threw back. "Do you think you and Caleb can run this place alone? Just the two of you without Liza or me?" His dark brow came down. "You need us, Bryant. It's about time you admitted it."

Another stare down and Bryant strode out of the cabin, the door flying back to thud against the doorframe.

Liza let out a trembling breath. She found a chair and sank into it. Her knees were shaking, her insides quivering. "Thank you, Harvey," she stammered. "I never expected you to side with me."

He came to the table and sat. "I didn't either. I never figured it would come to that."

"Garrett is a good man," Liza said, strength returning to her. "He's an honorable Christian man. Not just a churchgoer, but a believer. I love him, Harvey."

"Yeah, it's a joke, isn't it? A weird, ironic joke."

Pulling at the buttons on her coat, she stopped and looked at him. "Are you talking about me and Garrett? Because if you are . . ."

He shook his head. "Not you. Me." He slicked down his black hair where it curled up in the back. "I may as well confess. It's going to come out anyway." He met her eyes. "It's Charlene. I'm crazy about her."

"I knew it," she said.

He scoffed. "Was it that obvious?"

She chuckled. "Only as obvious as a red shirt in a hospital ward."

He leaned back in his chair and stared at the ceiling.

"Don't worry," she told him. "I don't think she noticed it. I didn't see any signs from her, anyway." She reached out to clasp his arm to get his full attention. "She's a Christian now, Harvey. That means she's a changed person. It also means she shouldn't be in company with an unbeliever."

He met her eyes, unblinking.

"I've never asked you before," she went on, "but how do you stand with the Lord? Have you ever admitted you are a sinner and received Christ?"

He swallowed. "I've never told anyone about it, sis, but we went to a brush arbor with Mama when I was twelve and I asked Christ to save me just sitting there on the bench." He looked regretful. "I was afraid that Pa and the boys would laugh at me if I let on that I was a Christian."

"But those philosophy books," she said. "Why do you read them and not the Bible?"

"Who said I don't read the Bible?" he asked. "I've been reading the Bible and comparing it to what those men teach. They are way off the beam, I tell you. Paine worst of all." He leaned toward her. "I want to go to a good, strong Christian university where I can learn to speak out against all that hooey those 'learned men' are spouting."

"Harvey! I never dreamed . . ."

He cut her off. "Do you suppose Garrett would let me call on Charlene sometime?"

"I don't see why not. She's only working there. She can see whomever she pleases."

"She's the sweetest gal I've ever met, Liza

— hardworking, kind, and sensitive. She's got a humility about her none of the church girls around here have."

"More power to you, Harv," she said. "We may both end up over there. From what Garrett tells me, it wouldn't be such a bad thing either." She got up to hang up her coat and clear away the remains of dinner, still spread out on the table.

Harvey returned to the loft. She was left alone until Bryant and Caleb came in half an hour later. By that time it was full dark. Caleb sent her several dark looks, but Bryant didn't glance her way once. They sat in the sitting room before the fireplace for a few minutes, then climbed to their beds.

A few minutes later, Liza gratefully closed her bedroom door behind her, relieved to be alone within her own sanctuary. What a day it had been: so many conversations to remember, so much new information to process.

Pulling on her warmest gown and nightcap, she slipped into a double layer of wool socks and pulled the quilt around her ears. She was looking forward to meeting Garrett's people. From what she had seen so far, they were a wholesome group, one she could be proud to be a part of.

Excitement and exhaustion finally won

out, and she fell into a deep sleep.

Liza awakened to find a dim stream of light pouring through her window. Blinking, she tried to make her mind focus. Suddenly, it hit her. Breakfast was late.

She flung back the covers and dashed into the kitchen. Crumbs of bread crust on the table and the remains of coffee told the story. The men had eaten a cold breakfast and started their day without waking her.

Her heart sank. It was a sign of Bryant's disapproval. Normally, he would have called her if she wasn't in the kitchen when he came down.

She cleared away the few dishes and set a pot of stew on the stove. As soon as she finished, she headed for the loft ladder. Her biggest fear about Bryant's disfavor was that he would ask her to leave before she had a chance to look for a box of letters.

The loft was a second floor that covered the entire span of the house with a three-foot square opening for the ladder. With only four windows, it was always a little dark unless the summer sun streamed through it — a rare happening.

The small door to the storage room had cracked leather hinges that were so dry the door was difficult to move. Inside, the windowless area was too dark to see much. She had to find a lantern in the boys' quarters and return with it to begin a search.

Old trunks, forgotten pieces of broken furniture, wooden crates — all covered with thick dust and cobwebs. Liza shrank away as her face brushed a spider web.

Leaving for a second time, she found a kerchief to completely cover her head. Bringing a broom this time, she knocked down every cobweb she could see and looked more closely.

She searched for almost an hour and found nothing. In the far back corner of the room, deep in the shadows, a wooden crate held a box made of thick paper and tied with twine. Liza pounced on it.

Moving to a three-legged table propped on two crates, she pulled off the twine and peered inside. It was full of letters in chunky handwriting, the ink thick and dark. The envelopes were all addressed to Priscilla Wainright.

Quickly, Liza replaced the lid on the box and hurried out, returning the lantern and closing the groaning door behind her.

She checked the stew pot as she passed through the kitchen, then hurried to her room to spread the letters on her quilt. Getting comfortable on the bed, she sorted the envelopes according to the writer. There were five in all, but most of the letters by far had come from someone who signed her name Suzanna, Priscilla's sister. Organizing the letters by date, she read each one.

The writer was Suzanna Mayfield. She lived in Granite City, Oklahoma, where her husband, Alexander, owned the *Bugle,* a local newspaper. She had five children. One of them was a late-comer, a little girl named Magdalene who was born when the oldest was seventeen.

When Liza reached a letter dated December 30, 1833, her hands began to tremble as she read:

Dear Priscilla,

I'm so sorry about the trouble with your boys. They can be difficult when they reach a certain age. I can tell you from experience now that my David has reached twenty. He's a sweet boy, no doubt, but so determined. I guess it is part of coming of age, not that we mothers like to see it happen.

I wish there were some way that I could relieve your mind. All I can say is that time heals wounds. I hope that is true in your case.

After that she moved on to her own news.

Holding the letter, Liza considered. If Suzanna's husband had owned a newspaper, maybe his sons took it over after he died. It was a place to begin anyway. She scanned the rest of the mail but found nothing of interest. Keeping out that one letter, she packed everything neatly into the box once more and took it back to the storage room.

Intent on returning the box to its original place, she held the lantern high in one hand and had the box under her arm. She was about to replace it when she realized that there was a second box under the first. This one was dark and crumpled with no lid. Inside lay a dozen or more small books with their crumbling bindings upward.

Intrigued, Liza set down both lantern and letter box. She lifted one of the books and opened it. The leather crackled under her hands. The pages were yellowed and crumbled along the edges wherever she touched.

The first one had the following inscription on the first page: Private Journal of Priscilla Cartwell Wainright, 1855–1857.

Liza gasped. This was more than she'd ever hoped. Had Priscilla kept a diary in 1833? She dug through the diaries, checking the dates, and finally found the one she was looking for. She quickly turned to the ending pages of the book and read the entry for Christmas Day. It said basically the same thing as the story Johanna told, about the missing locket and Ryan's accusation of Jacob.

Disappointed, she turned back a few pages and read about Christmas preparations. Then on November 23, she found something interesting:

My sister, Suzanne, two of her sons, and her daughter came to visit today from Granite City. I was scared to death to have them traveling this time of year, but Suzanne insisted. Her husband had to travel to Europe on business, and she couldn't stand to be at home alone over the holiday.
Their little daughter, Magdalene, is so sweet. She's a handful at times, full of questions and so curious about her surroundings. They're planning to stay right through Christmas. I'm so glad to have Suzanne with me, especially since I've been feeling poorly for the past few weeks.

Liza read through to Christmas and then read that entry again. One phrase caught her eye. It had been meaningless before: "We caught Magdalene up in the loft this morning. How she managed to climb the ladder without falling, I'll never know."

So, there had been someone else in the loft that day. Changing her mind about returning the box of letters, she picked up both boxes this time and carefully climbed down to the first floor. She hid them under her bed, pushed far up against the wall.

Suddenly, she realized that she was starving. It was near noon and she hadn't eaten a single bite today.

Tomorrow at dusk, she was to meet Garrett. If only she could get word to him to meet her today instead. How could she live another whole day before she could tell him what she had found?

She was finishing the last bite of a cold bacon-and-biscuit sandwich when Harvey came in. He paused inside the door and then slowly closed it after himself. "Bryant's in a cold fury, Liza," he said. "I'm not sure how long either of us can stay here with him like that. He's nigh impossible to work with."

"Where is he now?" she asked, getting up to pour him some coffee.

"In the canyon. He had Caleb pack them some lunch, so they probably won't be back until later this afternoon."

She set the coffee before him. "Harvey,

how would you like to ride over to the Anderson ranch?" she asked, making him two bacon-and-biscuit sandwiches. "I just found out something about the feud, and I need to speak to Garrett."

"The feud?" he asked. "What are you up to now?"

Without answering, she swallowed the last drop of her coffee, then headed for her bedroom to change into riding clothes. "I'll tell you on the way," she said. "Eat your lunch so we can leave. We must be back before Bryant and Caleb come home."

Chapter 10

The Anderson ranch was surrounded by a whitewashed board fence that glowed brilliantly under the winter sun. As Harvey and Liza drew near the house, horse stables came into view, also whitewashed and clean. Paddocks and riding paths crisscrossed the wet fields like a maze. Everything was tight and strong, well-formed and well-maintained.

The riders drew up a moment to survey the place before they rode in. "I never dreamed it would look like this," Liza breathed.

He grunted. "Me neither. I've always considered the Andersons beneath us. Now I'm wondering which of us is the poor cousin." He urged his sorrel mare forward.

The ranch house was a two-story structure with a wide verandah on each level. It was as wide as it was deep, forming a cube shape with two chimneys on the east side and two more on the west. It was the biggest house Liza had ever seen.

Suddenly, she wondered if she should have come.

Before she could voice her fears to Harvey, Garrett came bounding from the house to meet them. He raised his arms to Liza to help her down, laughing in delight. "So, you couldn't stay away from me!" he said, his face glowing. He glanced at Harvey, still in the saddle. "Come on in, Harvey. Mother wants to meet the both of you."

Putting his arm about Liza's shoulders, he started toward the house with her.

She glanced back to be sure that Harvey was behind them.

That he was, peering toward the house as though searching for something.

Before they reached the front steps, Sarah Anderson came out to the verandah. She was a small woman with dark glossy hair pulled back into a bun low on her neck. She wore a full-skirted gown with a small white shawl pinned about her shoulders.

"Mother, this is Liza," Garrett called when they reached the steps.

Liza waited to speak until they reached the porch floor. "Good afternoon, Mrs. Anderson," she said.

"How good of you to come," Sarah said

warmly, reaching for Liza's hand. "I'm so glad to meet you." She turned to Harvey. "And this is . . ."

"Harvey Wainright," Garrett said. "The second brother."

"How do you do, ma'am," he said, his Adam's apple bobbing.

"Please come inside where it's warm." Sarah opened the door and led the way inside. "Charlene," she called when she stepped through the door, "please bring us some coffee." She turned to Liza. "Or would you prefer tea, my dear?"

"Coffee is fine," Liza said.

Inside the front double doors, they entered a wide hallway that ran the entire length of the house. To the left was a formal dining room and to the right a parlor complete with Belcher furniture and a massive gilt-framed mirror over the fireplace.

Sarah Anderson moved into the parlor and sat in a chair beside the hearth.

Overcome by the size of the room and the richness of the furnishings, Liza stopped on the threshold until Garrett's arm about her urged her inside. He led her to the red-velvet sofa and sat down. She sat, too, and rubbed her right hand over the soft fabric beside her.

Harvey found a chair and sank into it, his

head turned to watch the doorway.

Sarah made polite inquiries about Liza's health and the welfare of her family while they waited for the coffee to arrive.

When Charlene appeared, Harvey's face lit up.

The china cups on the silver tray rattled when she caught sight of him. Seconds later, she recovered herself and served the drinks.

"So, what brings you here?" Garrett asked when Charlene had returned to her duties elsewhere. "I know this isn't a social call."

Liza blurted out, "I found Priscilla's diary in the loft. I couldn't wait to tell you."

"How wonderful!" Sarah said. She was genuinely pleased, and that surprised Liza a little.

"I brought it with me," Liza said. "It's in the saddlebag. I forgot to bring it in."

"I'll fetch it," Harvey said, getting to his feet. He strode out and closed the door behind him.

"There were visitors in the house when the locket disappeared," Liza went on. "Priscilla's sister, Suzanne, and some of her family came for Christmas that year. Two sons and a little girl about three years old named Magdalene came with her. The little girl managed to climb the loft steps and scared them all because she could have fallen and hurt herself."

She turned to Garrett. "Suzanne's husband, Alexander Mayfield, owned the *Bugle* in Granite City, Oklahoma. We could trace the family from that, couldn't we?"

"We could, but I think we'd have to travel to the town."

Sarah said, "Why not send a telegram to the courthouse there asking for information about Magdalene Mayfield and her brothers? That would save you a possibly useless trip."

"That's a good idea, Mother," he said.

He turned to Liza. "Wouldn't Suzanne's sons have slept in the loft?"

Liza said, "More than likely, they did."

"One way or the other," he replied, "we need to find any of those children and learn if they know anything more."

"I wonder where Harvey is," Liza said, looking toward the door.

Garrett quirked in one side of his expressive mouth. "He'll turn up when he's ready to, I reckon."

Holding her cup near her lips, Sarah looked thoughtful. "I wonder why no one ever considered that someone else in the house could have taken the locket instead of Jacob. Why did Ryan accuse him exclusively?" She sipped her drink.

Garrett set his cup down and replied, "Probably the jealousy between them."

Liza added, "He would also hesitate to accuse one of his cousins, I imagine."

Sarah shook her dainty head. "As godly as Ryan was in his later years, he had that one Achilles heel. He could never forgive Jacob. So much turmoil has come into the lives of so many because of that one fault."

"Lest any root of bitterness . . ." Garrett said.

Liza added, "Unfortunately, the people in our generation are the many who are defiled." She gazed into Garrett's face. "I hope we can break the cycle of hurt. It seems to grow with each new branch on the family tree."

"That's our prayer, too," Sarah agreed. "I hope you young people can put an end to it all."

Finally, Harvey reappeared carrying the decaying journal. They spent the next thirty minutes reading the entries aloud and discussing them.

Finally, reluctantly, Liza said, "We've got to be heading home. If we don't leave right away, Bryant and Caleb will get back to the house, and we won't be there."

"How is that situation going?" Garrett asked.

Harvey scoffed. "About as bad as it can get. I don't know how much longer I'm going to be able to work with Bryant. He's as prickly as an old cactus. And Caleb takes Bryant's side in everything. He always has."

Sarah stood, and they all followed her lead toward the door. "If things get too difficult for you," she said, "you are both welcome here."

Garrett grinned at Liza. "More than welcome."

Harvey stepped forward to shake Sarah's outstretched hand. "Thank you, Mrs. Anderson," he said, a hearty note in his voice.

"Yes, thank you," Liza said. She came closer to take Sarah's hand, but the older woman drew her into a hug. "You're as sweet as Garrett described you," she said. "I'm awfully glad to know you. Please come back any time you are able."

The warmth of Sarah Anderson's acceptance and approval spread through Liza and brought a glow to her face. "Thank you, ma'am. I'm so glad I came."

Without time for long good-byes, they were quickly back in the saddle and trotting down the trail.

On the ride home, Harvey remarked, "That was quite a different picture than we've been painted, isn't it, Liza?"

"Totally different," she agreed. "I'm only sorry that we didn't venture over there sooner."

"I'm sure Garrett is, too," he said wryly.

"Say, what about you and Charlene?" she demanded. "You were gone an awfully long time getting that book."

His lips came out as he tried to stifle a smile. "We're going to sit together in church next Sunday," he said smugly.

"Harvey!" she gasped. "Garrett and I are just now getting to that point. Are you sure you're ready for that?"

He kept his gaze straight ahead. His voice was dry. "I've never been so sure of anything in my whole life."

The ranch yard was empty when they arrived home. Liza helped Harvey tend to the horses so they could be turned into the corral as soon as possible, and then she hurried to the house to get supper finished. Whipping up a small pan of biscuits, she stirred the stew and added a hint of salt. She brought a leftover dried-apple pie from cold storage and set it on the back of the stove to warm it.

She had arranged to meet Garrett the following evening to plan their next move. If they had to travel to Oklahoma, they shouldn't travel alone. It was too far to venture without a chaperone. Who could they get to go along? Harvey was needed at home.

At the edge of dark, Bryant and Caleb rode into the yard. They took their time coming to the house, and when they entered, their faces were rigid. They ate their food in disapproving silence, then retired to the loft.

Liza was relieved to hear their boots on the floorboards overhead.

Harvey found a book in the sitting room and sat near the hearth to read by lamplight.

Liza finished washing up the dishes and closed herself in her room. She slowly changed for bed and brushed out her waist-length hair. Mrs. Anderson might have to make good on her promise to take them in. Liza wasn't sure how much more of the ice treatment she could take from those boys. She certainly wasn't going to tolerate being made to feel unwelcome in her own home.

The next day, Liza set to cleaning the cabin like a winged fury. Scrubbing the last speck of mud from the floors, including both porches, she cleaned the hearth and polished every surface in the kitchen. Reorganizing the pantry after lunch, she kept one eye on the clock. She had to meet Garrett at the big tree this afternoon.

Finally, it was time to go.

As before, he was already waiting for her there. Pulling her behind the tree, he kissed her soundly and held her close. "It seems like forever since I saw you last," he said. "We've got to put an end to this distance between us."

She giggled, breathless. "It's not more than a mile," she said.

"Ten feet is too much for me." He kissed her again.

"Garrett, what did you decide?" she asked when she could speak again. She couldn't linger here too long.

"I sent a telegram to Granite City asking for information about Magdalene or her brothers. So, now we'll play a waiting game until they answer."

"How long?"

"It could be one day . . . or a week. There's no way of knowing," he replied. "I'm going to ride to town every morning to see if an answer has come."

He kissed her nose. "I guess we'll have to meet here every afternoon until then."

She shook her head, regretfully. "I'm afraid I can't do that. If Bryant and Caleb come in early, I won't be able to get away. That's bound to happen soon."

"If you don't come, I'll sneak around behind the cabin and tap on the window at the back porch."

"Garrett, I'm afraid. Bryant could start shooting and claim he thought you were a prowler or a thief."

"That's not likely. I doubt he'd take a chance on hanging for it."

She sighed. "Last night, neither Bryant nor Caleb spoke a word to Harvey and me when they came in. They gulped down their suppers while they glowered at us and then went straight up to bed."

He squeezed her to him. "I can't stand to think of you having to put up with that."

"At least he isn't threatening me," she replied. "Not yet, anyway. I'm afraid one of these days he's going to come home and order Harvey and me to pack our things."

"That wouldn't be such a disaster, would it?" he asked, smiling down at her. Looking deeply into her hazel eyes, he grew sober. "Just as soon as we can try to set things straight with your brothers, I want you to marry me."

"What if Bryant won't listen?" she asked.

"Honey, I said *try* to make amends. Whether he accepts what we say or not, I still want you to marry me." He searched her face. "Will you do it, Liza? Do you love me at all?"

"I do love you," she whispered, a cold knot of dread in her throat. "But I love them, too." She leaned her forehead against his chest. "What am I going to do?"

Chapter 11

Two days later, Garrett was waiting for her, a yellow page in his hands. When she reined in Sassy, he waved it at her.

"It came yesterday," he said. "I picked it up this morning."

Swinging down, she said, "What does it say?"

Grinning, he shoved it at her. "Here. Read it."

She scanned the page then went back to read it more closely.

Garrett hovered over her, watching her face.

> Scott Mayfield current owner of *Bugle,* grandson of Alex M. STOP Family still in Granite City STOP Invite you to come for a visit STOP Telegram your arrival date to SM before coming STOP

"When can we go?" she asked.

He took her hand and leaned against the

tree's massive trunk. "We can't go alone," he said, "and Bryant would have to know you'd be away for two or three days."

She nodded. "I can take care of the second part, but what about the first? Harvey can't come. He's got to help at the ranch."

"Mother says she can spare Charlene for a couple of days. What would you say to Charlene coming?"

"I'd be delighted," she said. "I'd like to get to know her better."

"It's settled." He lifted her hand to his lips. "I've got to run, my love. So many things to do before we go."

"But when?" she said with a laugh. "When do we leave?"

He chuckled. "Didn't I tell you? At daybreak tomorrow. The train leaves Wiley's Corner at seven o'clock."

After a quick and excited good-bye, Liza returned to the cabin. When she stepped inside, Bryant was at the kitchen table, a coffee cup in front of him. He stood when he saw her.

"Where have you been?" he demanded harshly.

"Down the road a mite," she said, closing the door firmly behind her. She took off her coat and hat. "I've been to see Garrett," she added when she was ready.

His scowl deepened. "You insist on defying me. What do you hope to gain by it?"

With calmness she didn't know she had, she met his stormy gaze. "I'm going to uncover the truth about what caused this bad blood between us and the Andersons," she told him. "I'm going to find out, and I'm going to put it to rest. For fifty years we've hated each other, but no one even knows why. There's something very wrong about that, Bryant."

"There's something very wrong about ignoring your elders," he retorted.

"My elders?" she demanded, heat rising in her. "You're fifteen months older than I am, in case you've forgotten." Shoulders squared, chin high, she took two steps toward him. "You're not the old man of the family! We're a team. We all have a say, and we all work equally hard. That's what we agreed to when Pa and Ma died."

His expression remained like flint.

She went on. "I'm going on a train trip with Charlene and Garrett. We're leaving in the morning, and we may be gone for three days."

"If you go, Liza, don't bother to come back. I'm warning you."

She felt that old fear rising, but she pushed it back. "There was a family visiting here the day the locket disappeared," she said.

"What locket?"

Caleb came in and closed the door. He stood just inside without moving to even remove his coat.

"This entire fight was caused because Ryan Anderson lost his mother's locket. It was all he had left of her. After both his had parents died, he was the foster son of the Wainrights. He and our grandfather, Jacob Wainright, were about the same age. There was jealousy between them. When the locket came up missing, Ryan accused Jacob of taking it for spite. Jacob hotly denied it, but the mystery was never solved. No one found the locket."

Caleb's chest swelled. "My grandfather was no common thief!"

She turned to him for a second. "That's what I'm trying to prove! Don't you see? If I can prove that Jacob was innocent, then we can forget the whole thing. Garrett and his mother are willing to forgive and forget."

Harvey came in at that point. He sized up the situation and moved three steps into the kitchen where he could see everyone at once.

"Where are you going?" Bryant asked.

"Granite City, Oklahoma. It's just across

the border from Colorado, not far from Boise City. I'll be gone for two days, possibly three if we can't find the right person. There must be someone in the Mayfield family who's old enough to remember that day. It was exactly forty-nine years ago, Bryant. They'd be grandparents or great-grandparents by now. There's not a day to lose."

"You're grabbing at straws," Bryant scoffed.

"What will it hurt to try to find the truth? We may just clear our family name." She flung both hands out to him. "We've been living under the shadow of that accusation long enough. Don't you think it's time to give our family a clean slate?"

"She's right," Caleb said, his chin lifting a little. "I want to know what happened."

"So do I," Harvey added.

Hearing Harvey's voice, Bryant's gaze fastened on him. "And you! You're in on this, too. I can smell it." His mouth formed a grim line. "That's what too much book learning does to a man. Makes him *weak*." His face twisted as though he had tasted something disgusting.

Harvey swelled up. "Oh, so hating someone without knowing why is a sign of strength, is it? Turning on your own blood kin because of something that happened half a century ago is strong, too, I suppose." His chin tightened. "I'm sorry, Bryant. You've got it wrong. It takes guts to step out of the mold and stop the course of things. Letting things run their course is *easy.*"

For a moment, Liza feared they'd come to blows, but then Bryant backed off. He pinned Liza with his dark gaze. "Go," he said, "but take Harvey with you. I'll not have my sister going off with a man for days at a time without a brother with her."

Liza said, "But the stock . . ."

"We'll take care of it," Caleb put in. "Go ahead, Liza. Maybe you can get this whole ugly mess settled. I'm tired of it. It's time things got back to normal around here."

She glanced at Harvey. "We leave at daybreak. The train leaves Wiley's Corner at seven."

He nodded, then hustled toward the door. "In that case, I've got some stuff to take care of before nightfall." He grasped the latch and went out.

Liza took off her coat and hung it up, ignoring the still forms of her brothers. Were they frozen like that? Why couldn't they go outside or sit by the fire?

Finally, Bryant moved into the sitting

room. "How about some checkers, Caleb?" he asked, his voice surprisingly mild. "I brought the game back to the house last night."

"Sure." The youngest brother hurried out of his coat and sat across from Bryant near the fireplace.

Heartsick at the growing void between herself and her boys, Liza checked the roast in the oven and stirred the pot of beans on the back of the stove. Despite the pain they caused her, those boys were everything to her. Was there any way to keep the family together?

That evening, she knelt beside her bed, her knees on the icy floor. "Oh, Lord," she prayed aloud, "I believe You brought Garrett into our lives to settle this awful feud. Please make a way of peace between our houses and between my brothers and me." She got up and crawled between the frigid sheets, shivering and waiting for the bed to grow warm. How would she ever be able to sleep?

The next thing she knew, Harvey's call came through her door. "Liza!" he called, his voice husky. "We've got to be leaving. Are you up?"

Instantly awake, she threw back the covers and bolted upright. "I'll be there in a few minutes," she called. "Make some coffee, will you?"

Twenty minutes later, they were in the saddle. Their breath came out in steamy billows as they talked.

"What about our horses?" Harvey asked. "We can't leave them tied to a tree for three days."

"Garrett will have thought of that," she said. She told him of the telegram and of their hopes for this trip. They talked of it for the entire ride.

When they reached the big oak, a buckboard and three people waited for them — Garrett, Charlene, and a young Hispanic boy about Caleb's age.

"Well, what do you know?" Harvey breathed when he saw Charlene.

"Sorry. I forgot to mention that she was coming," Liza said.

He didn't seem to mind at all.

Garrett came near. "Jorge will bring the buckboard back from town and take all the horses to our stables," he said, reaching for Liza to help her down. "We've got to hurry."

The men moved the cases into the waiting buckboard. Sitting on the bench seat with the ladies, Garrett held the reins while Jorge and Harvey climbed in back, then shook the leather straps and called to the twin blacks. They set off at a rumbling, lurching pace.

An hour later, the four young people were settled into facing plush seats, their faces gleaming with excitement.

Harvey laughed aloud. "Who would have ever imagined that we'd be traveling together today?" He grinned at Charlene beside him. "I'm not complaining."

Dressed in a dove-gray gown with a white crocheted collar, Charlene looked calm and at peace. Her bold stares and flashing glances had totally evaporated. With her clean-washed face and her hair drawn back into a bun, she could hardly be recognized as the same girl who had arrived at the Running W just days before.

As the car rattled down the rails, the day passed in quiet camaraderie. They reached the station at Granite City a little past four in the afternoon, then waited fifteen minutes in line before they could disembark from the train.

"Where to now?" Liza asked when they reached the platform. She wished for her woolen shawl that hung in her room. The icy wind cut like a knife.

"To the newspaper office," Garrett said. "I'll check at the station to see if we can hire a cab or rent a wagon." He set off and returned a few minutes later. "I found a cab driver. He'll take us to the *Bugle*."

At least it was a closed carriage. Her feet were still throbbing from cold, but getting out of the wind was a mercy. The four of them sat in nervous silence. Whatever they learned here would set in motion a course of action that would affect all of their lives.

A young, pock-faced clerk was about to lock the office door when they reached it. He opened the door a crack, waiting to hear their story.

"We've just arrived from Colorado to see Mr. Mayfield," Garrett said. "He's expecting us."

The young man pulled the door open and let them pass. His first words to them were, "Second door on the left down that hall." He pointed in the general direction with his sharp chin.

Walking single file through a warren of oak desks piled high with papers, the four young people found the office. Garrett knocked on the door.

A woman's voice called, "Come in, please," and they entered a waiting room with six wooden chairs in formation along the west wall. The secretary was a matronly woman with a blond-gray pompadour hairdo. "Yes? May I help you?" she asked in cultured tones.

Garrett replied, "We're here to see Mr. Scott Mayfield. We're relatives of his just come from Colorado." He introduced each one in the party.

After a few minutes of fuss and bother, she returned to say, "He will see you now."

Mayfield's office was tastefully done in dark wood and darker leather, the furniture well turned out, the artwork refined. However, every level surface was covered with papers, most of them newsprint in some form of production. One wall held a bulletin board with paste-up squares covering it.

Mayfield himself was a short, round man with a bald head the shape of a mosque dome. He seemed worried. When he came to greet them, he offered an apologetic smile. "I'm glad to meet you," he said and carefully got each of their names. "You're like a vision from the past."

"We're here on a mission," Garrett told him. "We were wondering if you could answer some questions."

"Here, sit down." He moved some piles to form an awkward stack on the floor in front of his desk.

When they found seats, he returned to his own desk chair and Garrett continued.

"The event we're here about happened on Christmas Day of 1833 at the Wainright cabin. From what we can gather, some members of your family were there for the holiday."

He frowned and his bald head creased high above his eyes. "In '33 I would have been . . . twelve years old. Let me see . . ." He stroked his thick neck and squinted at the pressed tin ceiling.

Liza gave him a few minutes then said, "Your little sister, Magdalene, climbed the loft stairs and gave everyone a fright. She was three years old."

His mouth fell open. "Right! We spent most of the visit riding in the corral with Jacob and Ryan. It was bitter cold, but you know how boys are. They don't have sense enough to come in when they should."

"Mr. Mayfield," Garrett said, "this is very important. Do you remember anything about a lost locket that day?"

Still frowning, he slowly nodded. "As I recall, Ryan was in a temper over it. It spoiled the end of our holiday. No more riding, no more checker games. Neither of the boys would pay my brother Fred or me the slightest mind after that. It ruined everything."

"Did you see the locket?" Harvey asked.

Mayfield shook his head. "Not once."

"Who slept in the loft?" Liza asked.

"Fred and me . . . and the other two boys, of course."

Garrett leaned forward, his face intent. "What about Fred?" he asked. "Would he know anything?"

Scott Mayfield shook his head. "Freddy was killed at Gettysburg," he said.

After a moment of awkward silence, Garrett said, "I'm sorry to hear that. We had no idea." He went on. "Does Magdalene live nearby? Would she mind seeing us, do you think?"

Mayfield's face cleared. "She'd be delighted. Family, no matter how distant, is a thrill to her. She lives on Haygood Avenue, six blocks from here. Her name is Dixon now. She's been a widow for fifteen years."

He wrote on a scrap of paper and handed it to Garrett. "Here is her address. Head east on this street for two blocks, then turn left on Haygood and go down four more blocks. Her house is on the left, white with a huge porch."

Garrett shook the little man's hand. "It's good to know you," he said. "Thank you for your help."

"I'm afraid I didn't help at all," he said, shaking hands all around. "Please do me a favor and tell Magdalene that I'll stop in on her later this evening."

They promised to do so and left. The same clerk let them out and quickly locked the door after them.

Holding her hat down to keep it from flying away, Liza clutched her overnight case in the other hand and hustled down the street after Garrett, whose long legs ate up the distance. She could hardly keep up.

Around the corner, they found Magdalene's house without a hitch, and Harvey knocked.

"I hope she's close by," Charlene groaned when a strong gust hit them.

The next moment, the door swung inward and a small woman appeared. She had brown hair with gold highlights in a high chignon, with no hint of gray despite her fifty-two years. Round cheeks and hazel eyes, she looked exactly like Liza with thirty-plus years added on.

The two women stared at each other for a short moment then Magdalene laughed. "I'm not exactly sure who you are, but we've got to be related," she said, moving back to let them in.

"I'm Liza Wainright," Liza said. "This is my brother, Harvey, and some friends, Garrett Anderson and Charlene Thomas."

"Anderson?" Magdalene asked. "Kin to Ryan Anderson?"

"He was my grandfather," Garrett said.

"I should have guessed it." She looked at each one. "The apple doesn't fall far from the tree, and that's a fact." She ushered them into her tiny parlor. "It's bitter out there. Would you like something hot to warm you up?"

When they gratefully accepted, she hurried out.

"Wow, that's Magdalene," Liza murmured. "Pinch me to make sure this is real. I *must* be dreaming."

Garrett pulled out his pocket watch. "At this rate, we may be able to head back home early in the morning."

Harvey grinned at Charlene but spoke to Garrett. "Don't hurry back on my account, old man," he said.

The older woman arrived with a tray and china cups. She handed everything around and set a plate of teacakes and sandwiches on the table.

The men and Charlene helped themselves.

Liza's stomach reminded her that she hadn't eaten since before dawn. She picked up half a sandwich and nibbled.

"So," their hostess said, sitting and spreading her full dark skirts about her, "what brings you to Granite City?"

Garrett repeated his story, ending with, "We came to ask if you might remember that day. I know you were very small. Honestly, we aren't holding out much hope that you can help us."

She nodded and the wisps of hair about her face swayed. "Of course I remember," she said. "How could I forget?"

"Did you see the lost locket?" Liza asked.

Tears filled the woman's eyes. For a moment, she didn't speak. Then she nodded. "I took it," she said.

Chapter 12

Sniffing, Magdalene pulled a handkerchief from her pocket and loudly blew her nose. "I found the locket in a small drawer, under some other things. My mama would have been furious if she caught me snooping like that. I would have gotten the spanking of my life. Even now, at fifty-two, I'm sure of it."

She paused to sip from her cup. "The locket was tiny and made of gold. It had a rose carved in the front of it. I'd never seen anything so lovely. I was mesmerized, and I hid under the bed to look at it where no one would see me." She paused, remembering.

"Mama started calling, 'Magdalene Esther Mayfield,' and I knew I had to go right away. I just dropped the locket under the bed and ran to the ladder." Her lips formed a wry smile. "I almost got spanked anyway, for climbing to the loft."

"Did you hear the boys arguing about the locket?" Garrett asked.

She nodded. "I watched the whole ugly scene, but I couldn't say anything. At three years old, the danger of a spanking outweighed every other thought in my childish head. We left the next day, and I've never mentioned that incident to a living soul since."

A tear spilled over. "I'm so sorry. How could you ever forgive me for the damage I've caused? Once I got older, I was too ashamed to admit that I'd covered up my part in that tragedy. It was so much easier to ignore what I had done."

Liza got up to hug her. "We didn't come to condemn you," she said, kneeling in front of the older woman's chair. "We came to set things right. Of course we forgive you." She glanced at Harvey.

He cleared his throat. "Yes, ma'am. We sure do."

Garrett added, "It was a child's folly. Please don't blame yourself anymore, Miss Mayfield."

"Maggie," she said, wiping her eyes. "Please call me Maggie."

She got up to hug each one in turn and say, "I'm sorry," another dozen times. Finally, she sat down again, exhausted.

"Maggie," Liza said, "which bed did you hide under? Do you remember?"

She blinked, thinking back. Her pixie nose was red, her eyes swollen. "There was a woodpile out the window beside the bed," she said. "Not that it's still there."

"But it is!" Harvey declared. "That's my bed now."

She focused on him. "You don't say! You still live in that cabin?"

They talked another hour, telling her of their families and their dreams until shadows filled the room.

"We must be going," Garrett said. "We've got to find a hotel for the night."

"A hotel?" Maggie demanded. "You're staying over with me. I won't have it any other way." She looked at the girls. "Would you mind helping me throw together some supper?"

"Oh," Liza said, "I just remembered. Mr. Mayfield at the *Bugle* said to tell you he'd be over later."

"Did he now?" she asked, beaming. "Scotti is my favorite brother. He spoils me terribly."

The rest of their visit was like a homecoming. Scotti Mayfield joined them for supper then left to bring his brother, Michael, and Maggie's two daughters to see their long-lost relatives. That evening the house was filled with people who were strangers but somehow very familiar — their looks, their mannerisms, even their opinions on certain matters.

The next morning, Maggie hugged each one of her guests. "God bless you, dear," she repeated four times in succession. She stood back so she could see them all. "You don't know what you've done for me," she said. "I feel like a thousand pounds just lifted off my back."

Liza smiled. "You've done a very brave thing, Maggie. You were honest. You could have sent us away, but you didn't."

The older woman's eyes filled with tears. "God bless you all!"

The young people filed out of the house and headed down the street. Garrett flagged down a cab, and they climbed aboard. The breeze was chilly but not as cold as it had been before.

The train ride home passed all too quickly. As the engine pulled into the Wiley's Corner station, Garrett whispered to Liza, close beside him, "I hate to send you back to that house, Liza."

She nodded. "I hate to go back," she admitted, "but it has to be." She squeezed his arm. "I just hope that Bryant will stop being angry long enough for Harvey and me to talk to him."

Garrett looked over at Harvey and Charlene, who were deep in their own private conversation. "How about if we pray before we get off the train?" he suggested, breaking into their tête-à-tête. "We need the Lord's help to get everything straightened out for the four of us."

Nodding, Harvey sat up a little straighter. "Good idea." He glanced at Liza. "I hate to think what Bryant's attitude will be when we get back."

Bowing, Garrett said, "Dear Lord, overshadow us all this day. Grant Your grace to face what is ahead and please have mercy to help us settle the angry spirit that moves among us. Bring glory to Your name, I pray. Amen."

Clasping Garrett's arm, Liza felt a lump forming in her throat. She was so blessed to have someone like Garrett watching over her. She was afraid to be so happy, lest something snatch it away and break her heart.

In a buckboard rented from the livery stable, they traveled to the Anderson ranch. Sarah and Charlene put together a quick supper for them, then Liza and Harvey set out for home.

At the end of their own long lane, Harvey remarked, "It's a shame we don't live further away. We're getting home way too soon for my taste."

Liza smiled at his foolishness. "I know what you mean, Harv, but we may as well get the showdown over with."

But when they reached the cabin, it was empty. There was no note and no signs of life. The kitchen was fairly clean, supper sitting cold in a pot on the lifeless stove.

Immediately they both set about building fires in the cook stove and fireplace. A few minutes later, the cabin felt the first hint of warmth.

"Do you think they decided to camp on the range?" Liza asked, worried. "It's bitter cold out there. What is Bryant thinking?"

Harvey scoffed. "I hope he gets cold enough to cool off his hot head." He added a fat log to the fireplace. "That should carry us through the night." Dusting off his hands, he moved to the foot of the ladder. "I'm tired. Unless you need something from me, I'll turn in now."

"Good night, Harvey," she said. "I'm going to do the same."

She went into her room, intending to retire, but once she got changed she was suddenly wide awake. Turning up the lamp beside her bed, she got down on her knees and pulled out the boxes hidden underneath. She had a detailed family history in those journals. Suddenly, it was imperative that she read them.

She pulled the quilts high around her and dumped the journals into her lap. There were more than a dozen of them. As she turned the box upright, she spotted a yellowed paper wedged into the bottom of it.

Carefully, she dislodged the document and held it up to the lamplight. At the top in curly script was: The Last Will and Testament of Matthew Zachary Wainright.

Liza's hands were trembling, and not only from the cold. She peered at the words of the will, reading them slowly, trying to decipher the legal jargon. Then one paragraph jumped out at her:

> The land holdings of the Running W, I leave to my sons, Jacob Wainright and Ryan Anderson, to be held in joint ownership by them and their heirs, providing that my wife, Priscilla Wainright, may choose to live in the cabin as long as she lives. The joint ownership will continue forever until both brothers or their heirs do willfully and voluntarily sign a bill of sale.

Liza read that section again and then a third time, forgetting the cold that was numbing her nose and the growing stiffness in her fingers. The Running W and the Anderson ranches were actually one large section. The fence was purely arbitrary. It meant nothing as far as ownership went.

She remembered Sarah Anderson's words: "I never could figure out why my father didn't sell his half of the ranch and go somewhere else. Why did he stay right here, neighbors with the Wainrights for the rest of his life?"

Ryan didn't sell because he couldn't sell. No wonder he was bitter against Jacob.

She refolded the will and sorted through the journals to begin reading at 1834. Scooting deeper into the covers, she held up the journals to catch the light until her arms grew weary and her eyes drifted closed.

The next thing she knew, it was morning. One of the books lay on the quilt near her head. The rest of them were in a heap to the side.

Blinking, she pushed her hair from her eyes. What a lazy dolt she'd become. She couldn't remember the last time she'd been in bed when the sun rose, and now she'd done it twice in just a few days.

She pulled on her robe and went to find Harvey. He was in the living room, sitting before the fire, gazing dreamily into it.

"What about the chores?" she asked.

"Done," he said, looking at her with a dull expression in his eyes.

"I'm sorry I slept so late. I was up reading . . ." She held up one finger. "Just a minute." Dashing into the cold bedroom, she found the will and brought it to Harvey. Pointing at the essential paragraph, she said, "Read here," and sat in the rocking chair while she waited.

He bent his head over the paper, progressing slowly through the flowery writing and dense jargon. Glancing up with a puzzled expression, he read it again. Finally, he laid the paper on his lap and focused on Liza. "We don't own the ranch free and clear," he announced. "The Andersons have joint ownership." He cocked his head. "Just wait until Bryant hears this. He'll turn to charcoal from the inside out."

"This is getting worse and worse," she said. "Would you mind eating cold biscuits this morning? There are a few in the tin on the counter. I want to look through the rest of those diaries to see what happened between Jacob and Ryan after Matthew died."

He folded the will and handed it back to her. "Make some coffee and I'll help you look through them," he said. "I'm not hungry anyway."

She suddenly smiled. "Lovesick, huh? Can't eat, can't sleep?"

He grimaced. "You should be talking, sis. I watched you and Garrett all the way to Granite City and back again."

She felt her cheeks growing warm. Turning toward the bedroom, she said, "I'll fetch those journals so you can start looking at them while coffee's brewing."

They pored over the journals dating from 1836 to 1845. They abruptly ended with an entry dated July 19.

Liza closed the last book. "Priscilla must have passed away sometime around then," she said. "She wrote all of this in the quiet of her own home, but what a treasure she left for us."

"She was a great lady," Harvey agreed. "I feel like I know her."

"Sarah had it right. Ryan did want to sell his half of the land and move away."

"But Jacob refused to sign."

"We still hold joint ownership, you know," Liza said. "The four of us and Garrett."

"I wish Grandpa Wainright had said a

majority instead of a unanimous agreement."

She stood to gather the books. "I've got to get busy. It's near noon. The house needs cleaning, and I haven't set anything on for supper yet."

"I'll help you until I have to go to the barn for the evening chores." Pulling on his coat, he filled both wood boxes and stoked both fires.

Liza put a roast in the oven, then stirred together bread dough. While it was rising, she peeled potatoes.

Harvey swept the cabin beginning at the fireplace hearth and ending at the back door.

Her paring knife whipping through a potato skin, Liza said, "Jacob was so offended at being falsely accused that he wouldn't speak to or even look at Ryan from then on."

"Can't you see Bryant doing that now?" he asked.

She grimaced. "I'm afraid I can. All too well."

Flipping the last of the dust onto a sheet of stiff paper, he tipped the paper over a metal trash can. "I wonder what happened to that locket," he said. "It was never found."

"Maggie said she dropped it under the bed and ran to the ladder. No one saw it after that."

"I'm going up there to look for it," he said, carrying the broom with him.

"It's not there," Liza called after him. "It couldn't be there after almost fifty years. Think of all the times the loft has been spring cleaned. I bet it got swept out years ago."

His voice sounded muffled when he called down. "There's no hurt in trying to find it. No one else has until now."

Fifteen minutes passed. Liza heard him shuffling around, the scraping of wood on wood a couple of times, then nothing.

"Liza," he called, "bring me a blunt knife, like you'd use to spread butter."

She dropped the last potato into the pot. "Give me a minute. I'll be right there." She set the pot on the stove and put on the lid. Picking up a table knife, she climbed the stairs.

Harvey was on his stomach with his face inches above the floorboards where his bed used to be.

"Wasn't the bedstead nailed in?" she asked.

"Yep. Old rusty nails. They didn't give me much trouble," he said, turning. "Did you bring that knife?"

She handed it to him.

Carefully, slowly, he slid the knife blade through the wide cracks in the floor, beginning at the wall and coming out four feet, then going back to the next crack.

Liza sat on the displaced bed, then soon lay down on it, her arm under her head, watching Harvey's slow progress. Her eyes drifted closed.

"Whoa!"

His shout brought her fully awake. She sat up. "What is it?"

Hunching over, he worked the knife back and forth a few times. "There's something wedged in a crack of the floorboards." He picked it up. "Look at this," he said. He handed her a black lump.

She rubbed it on her skirt and held it up to the window to catch the light. It was a heart shaped object no more than half an inch long with a string dangling from it. She looked closer. It wasn't a string, but a fine chain clogged with dirt. "Harvey!" she cried. She scrubbed the piece against her sleeve, turning it from one side to the other. A rose-shaped indentation appeared against a tarnished background.

Harvey knelt beside her to look at it.

"This is it! Look!" Holding it up for him

to see, she placed it in his outstretched hand, then flung her arms around him. "You found it! I can't believe it!"

Chapter 13

Harvey held her for a moment then spoke, his voice dry. "Not that it will do us any good."

Liza pulled back, her smile dimming. "You think Bryant won't care about this?"

"Bryant makes up his own mind, regardless of the facts," he declared. He moved to sit beside her on the bedstead. "But does that matter to us?" he asked. "We can make decisions just the same as he can, Liza. Why should his stubborn prejudice change our thinking or our plans?"

She nodded, her mouth sad. "I wish Caleb weren't so tied to him, though. I'm afraid we're going to lose Caleb, too."

He hugged her again. "Let's let the Lord take care of it for us," he told her. "If they don't come around now, then maybe they will sometime in the future." He gave her back the locket.

She shrugged and looked down at the

locket in her hands. "That's what Priscilla hoped, too. She died hoping that."

"Hey." He shook her gently. "This isn't a funeral. We just made a miraculous discovery. Wait until the boys hear about it. Maybe they won't be as negative as you're thinking." He stood. "Meanwhile, I've got to get this bedstead back in place." He grinned down at her. "I may be strong, but I can't move it with you sitting on it."

She shot him a disbelieving look and swatted at him. He dodged, laughing. Smiling in spite of herself, she left him and headed for the ladder, the locket safely in her skirt pocket.

She returned to the kitchen to check on supper. A few moments later, a loud rapping sounded at the door. She jumped at the sound, then went to see who it was. Harvey shinnied down the ladder as she crossed the room.

She pulled the door open and her heart jumped when Garrett strode inside.

"What's wrong?" she asked, sure there must have been a catastrophe to bring him to her front door.

"I had to come and see if you're all right," he said. "Liza, I've got to get you away from here. I can't stand it. I'm worrying about you from dawn till midnight and losing sleep worrying about you after that." He clasped her hands. "Please come back with me."

"I can't come now," she said, "but that may change this afternoon. I've so much to tell you. Let's sit down."

They moved to the sofa before the fireplace, and Harvey sat in the chair nearby.

Liza glanced at Harvey as she reached into her pocket. "Look what Harvey found this afternoon," she said, pulling out the locket. She held it toward Garrett.

He peered at the blackened object and slowly reached for it. The chain slithered through his fingers and hung in two crooked, filthy lines below his hand. He turned the locket over several times. "Where was it?" he asked finally.

Harvey answered. "Under my bed where Maggie said she dropped it. It had fallen into a big crack between the floorboards and gotten covered with dirt."

Liza added, "It probably got swept into the crack by someone bending over to push a broom under there. The bedstead was nailed to the wall, so it was almost impossible to see what you're sweeping. And the loft is always a little dark."

He gathered the chain into his palm and hefted the tiny object. "It's so light. I can hardly feel it in my hand," he said. "To think this little thing caused so much grief."

"We have to show it to Bryant and Caleb," Liza said. "Depending on their reaction, Harvey and I may be going back with you this afternoon."

"That's not all we found," Harvey said.

Liza paused to look at him, a question on her face.

"The will," he said.

"Oh, I forgot about it! I was so excited about the locket." She ran to the bedroom and brought the yellow page out to Garrett. Pointing, she said, "Read this paragraph."

With his brow furrowed, Garrett bent over the paper. "Well, if that don't beat all," he said in a moment. "I had no idea our properties were tied together."

Harvey said, "That was Matthew Wainright's idea of forcing peace between the two boys, I guess." He shrugged. "Whatever it was, it didn't work."

"We need to get this legally undone," Garrett said. "If we all agree to divide the property between us, then we won't have to wait for everyone to sign again."

"What do you mean?" Harvey asked.

"There are five of us," Garrett said. "We can split the land up five ways. I suppose that will mean I'll have to give up some acreage in order to make it come out right, but I'm agreeable to that."

"What about your mother?" Liza asked.

"Pa left his claim to the property to me."

"Why didn't anyone explain all this to us?" Harvey exclaimed.

Garrett said, "Both of us lost our fathers in a sudden tragedy. They probably figured they had plenty of time to tell us how things stood." He looked from Harvey to Liza. "The Anderson-Wainright situation wasn't a topic for the dinner table, was it?"

Both of them shook their heads. "We never talked about it."

"Neither did we," Garrett said. "But now that we know, it's our responsibility to take care of it while we can."

"Now's the time to do it," Liza agreed. "If we don't deal with it now, the next generation will have many more people who have to sign off. It'll end up a hopeless tangle."

Garrett handed the will to Liza. "Put that back in a safe place. We have to take it to a lawyer as soon as possible."

She took the thick pages. "Would you like some coffee?" she asked.

"A glass of water," he said. "I'll come to the dining room, so I can talk to you while you're in the kitchen." He stood and handed her the locket, then paused by Harvey's chair. "How are you doing?" he asked.

Harvey stood. "Not too good, I'm afraid. Bryant is unbearable. I don't know what makes him so difficult."

"He's angry," Liza said, pumping water into a pitcher. "He always gets angry when he doesn't get his way."

Harvey looked out the window. "They're back early," he said. "Bryant's coming to the house, and Caleb is right behind him."

"I tied my horse in front of the house," Garrett said. "I'm tired of hiding around corners."

Harvey hitched his belt a little higher. "Let them come. It's time we had it out."

Liza's heart was thumping so hard she couldn't pour Garrett's water into a glass. She set down the pitcher and turned toward the door, leaning against the edge of the table.

Bryant shoved the door open and it hit the end of the kitchen counter with a bang. He stepped inside with his chest swelled, his hands curled at his sides.

Caleb came after him and closed the door.

For a moment no one spoke, then Liza said, "We found the locket, boys. It was in the loft where Maggie said it would be. She was right, Bryant. Jacob didn't take the locket. It was all a mistake."

Her brother's upper lip drew up. "What do you want me to do, Liza?" he fumed. "Shake hands and be best buddies? Well, it's not happening."

"There's more to it than that," Harvey added. "We found Matthew Wainright's will. You've got to look at it. It still affects all of us — all five of us in this room."

For the first time Bryant looked uncertain. "What does it say? Tell me."

Liza said, "Matthew Wainright tied the land up with a restriction that it can't be sold unless both Ryan Anderson and Jacob Wainright *or their heirs* all sign off on the bill of sale."

Harvey added, "We don't have two ranches. The Running W includes the Andersons' place. That fence is just smoke and mirrors, Bryant. They put it up the same way people hang a blanket down the center of a room. It keeps other folks out, but they're all still inside the same four walls."

Caleb moved to a chair. "Well, if that don't beat all," he drawled.

Bryant scowled at Harvey. "Well, it happens that I don't want to sell," he said.

Garrett spoke for the first time. "Neither do we. We only want to divide up the property, so each person can make a decision about what to do without having to wait for anyone else to agree." His voice softened. "In order to divide the entire section into five parts, I'm going to have to give up claim to some of my acreage. But I'm willing to do that, if it'll make peace between us."

Bryant scoffed. "You'll grow old holding out for that to happen, Anderson. Locket or not, you're still a . . ."

"Bryant!" Liza cried. "Stop it! I'll not have you talking to him that way." She stepped closer, her voice shrill. "I'm going to marry him, do you hear me? You can be miserable all you want, but that's not going to stop me from being happy." Tears ran down her face. "I don't know what I'll do without my boys," she sniffed, "but I've got to make my own choice about this."

Caleb stood and came to her. He looked back at Bryant. "I respect you as my oldest brother," he said, "but it's not right to make Liza's life a misery. Who else is she going to marry if she turns him down?"

Dashing the tears from her eyes, she tried to smile at Caleb. "I'm not marrying him because he's my last chance," she said. "I love him, Caleb." She started crying again. "But I love you, too!"

Caleb leaned over to hug her.

Bryant watched them. His expression remained the same, but something in his stance softened. "You can visit us, Liza," he said, "as long as you come alone." With a hostile look directed at Garrett, he stalked out of the house.

The tension in the room immediately relaxed.

"I don't want you to go," Caleb said. "Things have been pretty awful around here since you've been leaving us to go everywhere."

Liza hugged him again. "I'm not going anywhere right away," she said. "We'll work all of that out before the time comes." She blinked away the last traces of tears. "Anyone hungry?" she asked. "We missed lunch."

Garrett stayed around until Liza's three brothers left the cabin to do their chores. She was busy at the kitchen counter, washing up the last of the lunch dishes when they went out.

Without saying anything to her, Garrett came behind her and turned her around.

"I've got soapy hands," she said, laughing at him.

"We've got to talk," he said. The intense look in his eyes told her that he wasn't going to be put off.

She turned and quickly dipped her hands

in the rinse water. Grabbing a towel, she said, "What do we need to talk about?"

He pulled her into his arms. "It's about what you said to Bryant. I'm here to tell you that I'm holding you to it."

She looked doubtful. "What did I say?"

"That you were going to marry me." He kissed her. "I have to admit, I would rather you said that to me first, but I'm not that choosy. Just hearing you say it at all is good enough for me."

She melted into his arms for a long, sweet moment. "Garrett, is it ever going to be over?" she murmured.

Holding her close to his heart, he said, "Things will settle down after awhile, darling. Harvey and Caleb love you dearly. They're not going to count you as an enemy, not by a long shot. Even Bryant may come around eventually."

"I don't deserve you," she murmured. "You came up here with that loaded wagon like a gallant knight straight out of Harvey's Sir Walter Scott novels. I couldn't believe my eyes."

He took his time scanning her face. "I couldn't believe mine either. I thought an angel had come down to light on your front porch."

"An angel?" she retorted.

"Don't be so skeptical," he replied with a little laugh. "I *still* think so." He grew serious. "God brought us together, darling. I'm sure of it." He drew her closer for another kiss. His voice was husky when he said, near her ear, "Our romance may have begun with a train wreck, but believe me, it was no accident!"

Epilogue

The Rocking A Ranch
Wiley's Corner, Colorado
September 17, 1883

Dear Cousin Maggie,

It seems like so long since we've seen one another. I wanted to come to Granite City to give you this news in person, but I can't get away right now. There's so much to do. Garrett and I have set our wedding date for November 1. We do hope you and your family will be able to come.

Garrett wanted to get married last spring, but we were still in the middle of that legal muddle, and I wanted to wait until it was all settled. It's all over now, a mostly happy ending but a little sad.

The sad part is that Bryant has left us. After we discovered the locket, he moved his things into the bunkhouse and lived there for more than nine months. He still took his meals in the cabin, but he never talked to anyone besides Caleb. For a while, I was scared that Caleb would go out there with him, but he stayed in the house with us and slowly got to know Garrett. They're friends now.

It took us until spring to reach an agreement on dividing the land. Garrett's and my sections will be one ranch. Harvey's and Caleb's sections will be one ranch. Bryant got it into his head to leave, so he sold his rights to the rest of us for $1,000 each. He said he wants to go to Nebraska or Montana and build his own ranch. With $4,000, he'll have plenty to do that.

Now, for the good news. Harvey and Charlene are going to join us for a double wedding! Everything has worked out perfectly. I'm moving to Garrett's house and relieve his mother of overseeing the housekeeping staff. Charlene is moving into our cabin to take care of the boys. Harvey and Charlene have joined our little church, and they are so happy. Even Caleb is whistling these days.

We hope you can join us for the wedding. It would be wonderful to see you and your brothers and all their families there.

I remain your faithful cousin,
Liza Wainright

P.S. Please remember to pray for Bryant.

CHARLENE'S POOR MAN COOKIES

2 cups oatmeal
1 cup brown sugar
1/2 cup white sugar
1 cup flour
1/4 teaspoon salt
1 teaspoon baking soda
1/4 cup hot water
1/2 cup shortening, melted and cooled

Mix dry ingredients. Add wet ingredients. Mix well. Roll into 1-inch balls. Bake at 350° for 8–10 minutes. Makes about 3 dozen cookies.

The employees of Thorndike Press hope you have enjoyed this Large Print book. All our Thorndike, Wheeler, and Kennebec Large Print titles are designed for easy reading, and all our books are made to last. Other Thorndike Press Large Print books are available at your library, through selected bookstores, or directly from us.

For information about titles, please call:
(800) 223-1244

or visit our Web site at:
http://gale.cengage.com/thorndike

To share your comments, please write:
Publisher
Thorndike Press
295 Kennedy Memorial Drive
Waterville, ME 04901

WITHDRAWN